Winter Mythologies
and
Abbots

Winter Mythologies and *Abbots*

PIERRE MICHON

TRANSLATED BY ANN JEFFERSON

YALE UNIVERSITY PRESS ■ NEW HAVEN & LONDON

A MARGELLOS
WORLD REPUBLIC OF LETTERS BOOK

The Margellos World Republic of Letters is dedicated to making literary works from around the globe available in English through translation. It brings to the English-speaking world the work of leading poets, novelists, essayists, philosophers, and playwrights from Europe, Latin America, Africa, Asia, and the Middle East to stimulate international discourse and creative exchange.

Yale University Press books may be purchased in quantity for educational, business, or promotional use. For information, please e-mail sales.press@yale.edu (U.S. office) or sales@yaleup.co.uk (U.K. office).

Set in Electra and Nobel types by Keystone Typesetting, Inc.
Printed and bound by CPI Group (UK) Ltd, Croydon, CR0 4YY

Library of Congress Cataloging-in-Publication Data
Michon, Pierre, 1945–
    [Mythologies d'hiver. English]
    Winter mythologies and Abbots / Pierre Michon ; Translated by Ann Jefferson.
        pages   cm. — (The Margellos World Republic of Letters)
    "Originally published in two volumes as Mythologies d'hiver, copyright Éditions
Verdier, 1997, and Abbés, copyright Éditions Verdier, 2002."
    ISBN 978-0-300-17906-4 (alk. paper)
    I. Jefferson, Ann (Translator) II. Michon, Pierre, 1945– Abbés III. Title.
    PQ2673.I298M35413 2014   843'.914—dc23   2013020617

A catalogue record for this book is available from the British Library.

10 9 8 7 6 5 4 3 2 1

CONTENTS

ABBOTS

TRANSLATOR'S INTRODUCTION

Pierre Michon was born in 1945. He made his name with his first published work, *Vies minuscules* (Small Lives), which appeared in 1984, when he was thirty-nine. He is one of the finest and most admired French writers of today, and he has received recognition in the form of the Prix Décembre for *Abbots* and *Corps du roi* (The King's Body; a collection of short literary essays) in 2002, and the Grand Prix du Roman de l'Académie française for his novel *Les Onze* (The Eleven) in 2009. Another novel is in preparation, and he lives in Nantes.

Small Lives may have represented a late start for Michon, but it provided him with a theme on which a number of fruitful variations were to follow. Michon's preferred subjects are small in the sense of "obscure" or "apparently insignificant," and his preferred form is small in the sense of "short." *Small Lives* tells the stories of eight figures from Michon's own background in Creuse, part of the relatively poor and rural Limousin region, who positively or negatively shaped the vocation which, when finally realized, enabled him to restore them to life through his writing. The figures who populate *Winter Mythologies* and *Abbots* are for the most part equally obscure, though historically more distant: minor saints and little-known monks from the early Middle Ages in the French and Irish provinces. The brevity of the texts in which they appear gives readers the sense of merely glimpsing critical moments in these unfamiliar lives which often include or anticipate their end.

The origins of these tales lie in archives rather than in autobiographical experience or family legend, and although the pretext for writing them was for the most part a commission of some kind, Michon is at home in occasional pieces. The Alliance Française of Ireland commissioned the three texts which make up the first part of *Winter Mythologies* (1997); a writer's residency in the Vendée region was the basis for the trilogy of *Abbots*. Much of the material for "Nine Passages on the Causses" owes its origin to the chance find, in a village shop in Sainte-Énimie or Marjevols in the Causses region, of a reprint of a history of the Gévaudan first published in 1925. The two villages are themselves commemorated in the writing that resulted. Some of the sources are explicitly acknowledged, as they are in the opening sentence of each of the tales in *Abbots* or the references to the *Annals of the Four Masters*, while others, such as Gaston Phoebus's fourteenth-century treatise on the art of hunting, are more obliquely cited.

Michon's great theme is the precarious balance between belief and imposture, and the way the greatest aspirations can be complicated by physical desire or the equally urgent desire for what he calls glory. Brigid's fervor is as sexual as it is spiritual, but no less cogent for all that. Èble's monastery is founded as much on his desire to survive in the memory of men and on the blood that results from his sexual jealousy as it is on his religious convictions. Michon's abbots are politically savvy and skilled in manipulation. Édouard Martel's speleology and his discovery of some of the largest underground caves in France are portrayed as the direct result of personal ambition. Eloquence is born of an unfounded faith in a stolen relic which proves to be a fake. But faith can also be lost, as Michon's believers abruptly succumb to doubt, despair, or a destructive impulse that might, or might not, be the work of the devil.

The forms taken by religious belief in the Middle Ages may leave the modern reader incredulous, but the mix of ill-foundedness and spiritual ardor, conviction and ambition, are for Michon what makes literature possible in a secular world. Many of his monks and both his nineteenth-century positivists are writers: Martel ultimately creates his caves by naming their stalagmites and describing their size; Barthélémy Prunières draws as much satisfaction from the words with which he records his finds as he does from the discoveries themselves. Simon summons Énimie into being by instructing one of his monks to find written proof of her existence, and she is recalled to life once more when Bertran is commissioned to fabricate her legend. But to do so with his own kind of fictional truth.

Michon himself does nothing less. His characters derive their being partly from connections with Michon's own experience: his acquaintance with the places where they live, fatherhood, or the play with the name "Pierre," the author of the chronicle from which Michon takes much of his material for the trilogy. Just as important, like Énimie in Bertran's octo-syllabic poem, his characters also derive much of their being from the language he uses. Michon's is a language that is un-equivocally prose, in which a colloquial sarcasm and his own passing commentary can often be heard. But it also has a power-ful poetic component. This is first and foremost a matter of rhythm. His sentences are syntactically simple and often slightly elliptical, creating an impression of speed and abruptness or suggesting origins in ancient chronicles. Michon himself has said that this style is actually the result of his switch from pen to computer for composition. Then there is the poetry that Mi-chon conjures out of proper names—whether Celtic, medieval, or those of the islands off the Vendée coast (La Dune, Grues, La Dive, Elle) which speak in the original French of dunes, cranes, divinity, and a woman. There is poetry too in the rituals of religion or hunting, not to mention the Bible. The apparently incidental repetition of words and motifs creates a pattern that knits the small lives together as the devil and doubt come and go, figures are sliced in two through a variety of means, or the name "Hugues" settles on a number of awkward, fervent char-acters whose throbbing voice may be that of literature itself as it speaks in Michon's compelling miniatures.

Ann Jefferson

WINTER MYTHOLOGIES

We know from the teaching of the *Lotus Sūtra*
That the Bay of Naniwa in the province of Tsu
Is real too.
—JIEN, Tendai school, 12th century

Three Miracles in Ireland

BRIGID'S FERVOR

Muirchu the monk relates that Leary, king of Leinster, has three sweet young daughters. Brigid is the eldest. About the two others, the monk has knowledge only of their youth and their sweetness, not their names. Three young girls. It is daybreak in April in Dún Loaghaire, a town of wood and peat, which broods under the rule of a fortified clod. It's a royal town. The king is widowed and powerful, he is sleeping; he has thrown off his covers in the murky sleep of dawn. Brigid, who is awake, can see the river through the window under the first rays of the sun. She's a wise girl whose custom is to ask her father only for what her father cannot refuse her. She slips into the king's chamber, and before she sees that he is naked she has gently placed her hand on his shoulder. At her touch the king has a dream which agitates him the way a woman might. Brigid sees his agitation. He wakes. They look at each other like strangers, or husband and wife. Blushing, she asks his permission to bathe in the river with her sisters. He blushes and gives his consent.

All three girls run through the spring dawn. They reach the bottom of the embankment and throw their clothes under the foliage. Their little feet taste the water, and above their little feet their milk-white rust-spotted flesh is naked a hundred times over, the flesh of Ireland and of paganism. For the first time Brigid sees that this flesh is excessive, like a dreaming king. She laughs louder than her sisters. All three shriek when the cold bites their bellies; they slap the water with the palms of their hands, the birds fly up, and the hullabaloo reaches the road above.

Muirchu relates that along this road there is someone coming.

It is Patrick, archbishop of Armagh, the stateless Gaul, the miracle-worker, the founder. He is a graying colossus. A widower by vocation, and powerful. Behind him are thirty disciples and attendants with croziers and reliquaries, circular shields, books and swords. It is not entirely a stroll: if he is marching like this from Armagh to Clonmacnoise, from Armagh to Dún Ailinne, and from Armagh to Dún Loaghaire it's because he must convert to Christ the kings who in their fortified clods feebly worship Lug, Ogma, cauldrons, harps, and idols. And that, thinks Patrick on this spring road, is not difficult. All it requires is a few druidic spells, a couple of well-primed acolytes, and snow is instantly turned into butter, water into beer, the flames of purgatory appear at the tip of the magic rod, and the Holy Trinity in a shamrock leaf. These conjuring tricks are enough to bamboozle the jocular, pensive kings, who waver. And perhaps because he is growing old and his ardor and his malice are becoming blunted, Patrick regrets such facility as he walks along this road. He would like a real miracle to occur, just once, and for once in his lifetime, matter in its all its opacity to be converted to Grace before his eyes. He looks at the dust at his feet; he has not noticed that the road runs alongside a river. He hears the shrieks of the three girls.

He lifts his head; he sees the milk-white rust-spotted flesh through the leaves. The troop halts. He walks alone partway down the embankment. The girls are still at their games and do not know that the men are looking at them. Patrick immediately loves them with soul and body: they are flagrant and excessive, like Grace itself. He calls to them. Their gestures freeze. Against the morning sun they see silhouetted the powerful man who looks like a king: his linen tunic, his cloak, the gold on his clasp; and above him they see the royal procession, thirty attendants brought to a stand, croziers and shields, silence. Below this array the girls are naked. They offer greetings the way princesses greet a king, step unhurriedly onto the riverbank, and put on their clothes. He has come down and stands beside them; he is very tall. He asks whose daughters they are. He asks if they know the true God: they see that the gold on his clasp is a cross. They say that they do not know Him but that a slave has told them about Him, that they wish to know Him. They laugh; this beautiful morning has brought them a bathe, a king, and a god. They form a sort of pagan circle around the old colossus. They ask questions the way they slapped the surface of the water, the way they ran, with body and soul entire. "Is He handsome?" they say. "Is He young or old? Does He have daughters?" says Brigid. "Are his daughters beautiful, and are they loved by the men of this world?" Patrick replies that His beauty is devastating and that all the girls on this earth are His daughters. Although He is young, He has a son, but the Son is no younger than the Father, nor the Father older than the Son. He is the Bridegroom of every girl in this world.

The two sisters have sat down, but not Brigid. She has stepped a few paces away on the riverbank; she looks at her bare feet; she half turns her back to Patrick. She shivers. In a rasping voice she says, "I want to see Him."

"No one has seen Him," says Patrick, "who is not baptized." He talks about the River Jordan, the angels on its banks, the waters that redeem, about John and the Master. The girls want to be baptized. Once again they stand undressed in the river, very serious, their eyes closed. Patrick rolls up his chausses, and above this excessive flesh he performs the requisite small gestures. Brigid opens her eyes; the sun has turned; it is almost noon. "I don't see Him," she says.

King Leary's servants appear; he is worried about his daughters. A few words are exchanged. The procession leaves the river; they pass through the mantlet and the wattle surrounding the clod. The fortified gate closes on the croziers, the blessed colossus, and the girls: he clasps the two sisters close, holding them by the shoulders; Brigid walks ahead. Now they have disappeared from view. Patrick is doubtless performing his usual repertoire, devised for the benefit of the last of the feeble Merovingian kings. Leary's loud laugh can be heard, druidic spells, Latin. Preparations for a banquet can also be heard. Then, all night long, singing, inebriation. The girls are in their chamber.

Once again it is a spring dawn. Brigid at her window closes her eyes violently, and opens them: there is only the daylight gradually approaching, the silver thread of the river growing larger. The sun rises like a bridegroom, but it's not the Bridegroom. Gently she pushes open the door of the king's chamber. Wrapped in his fur-lined cloak Leary is sleeping like a drunkard, dreaming of raids and cattle. His mouth is open, he is older than he was yesterday, but brutal and handsome. He is talking in his sleep. He says a name. Brigid thinks she hears her own name in the name from the dream. All the blood leaps in her heart; she flees in panic down the passages; she is in the guest chamber. Patrick opens his eyes. Brigid is standing over him. She seems very tall. She is pale. She is excessive and determined like a queen. She says, "I want to see your God face to face."

Patrick sighs. He sits up on his bed.

Now we may imagine that all morning long and perhaps until nightfall, without leaving the guest chamber Patrick sits holding her in his gaze and evangelizes the girl, whose soul he sees naked just as he saw her milk-white rust-spotted breasts. All without druidic quibble, just the arid truth of the Greeks and the Jews; the Fall, which veils the holy Countenance from us, the oblique mirror in which fallen man can nonetheless glimpse the holy Countenance, and the promise that one day the veil will be torn away, a promise made to us on the banks of the River Jordan and repeated at a supper in Jerusalem. Brigid does or does not understand; but she understands only too well, and with painful clarity, that you sometimes see the face of God when you have received within your own body the body of the Bridegroom in the form of a little wafer that melts on the tongue. This is what she wants. And starting from that moment, on the following day and the days after that the colossus prepares the three virgins for communion, with the permission of the king, who, jocular or pensive, sometimes appears in the doorway of the room where Patrick is performing his holy pedagogical duties. Eight days, then: eight days of study and mortification, time for April to give way to May—and outside still the silver river where the girls no longer go. They learn Latin words from books, which they read by running their tiny fingers over them. Patrick's heart melts.

At last the eve of the ceremony arrives. They have tried on their white linen robes, the gold fibulas. They are asleep, except for Brigid. She is still wearing her robe and her fibula. She tiptoes into the king's chamber. It is lit by the moon. In the warmth of the May night, the king lies naked and quiet, at ease; he is not dreaming about women. Brigid wants to weep. And weeping she runs to the guest chamber. She kneels beside Patrick; he is sleeping somberly, and the sorrow caused by his dream is visible on his face. He dreams that Christ is dead, and Lord, how young the saints appear: they caress the naked body with their milk-white rust-spotted fingers. Brigid touches his shoulder; he sits bolt upright, afraid, and he is irritated by this indistinct fear. He can see the excessive flesh inside the white linen, he can smell it. "Swear to me," says Brigid, "that I shall see Him tomorrow." He looks at her with staring eyes, a large, irascible old man ejected from his dream back onto earth. He says, "You will see Him when you die, as will all of us in this world."

She is in the garden beneath the moonlight. She knows where she is going. She picks the red berries off the yew tree. They appear at the start of winter, and now, in the spring, they are always more concentrated and vicious, devastating. She crushes them and produces a small quantity of powder which fits in the hollow of her palm. Day is about to break. She goes back indoors, her fist clenched over the sombrous powder. The serving women have already brought the princesses' milk. Brigid opens her hand and the powder mixes with the milk.

They take communion in their white robes. Leary is there, wavering. He has combed his beard and donned his fur-lined cloak. They kneel, Patrick stands very tall above them, they receive the body of the Bridegroom from his hand. They are now in His presence, although He remains hidden. They have closed their eyes. Opening them, Brigid sees only the impassive face of the king. It is over. They step out into the May sunlight, and in the sunshine, one after the other, they fall to the ground: one on the steps, one on the path, and Brigid beside the rose-bush. One has her head in her arm, one in the dust of the track, Brigid is turned toward the sky, her eyes wide open. They are impeccably dead. They are contemplating the face of God.

COLUMBKILL'S SADNESS

Adamnan recounts that Saint Columba of Iona, who is still called Columbkill, Columbkill the Wolf—a member of the tribe of the northern O'Neills through his ancestor Niall of the Nine Hostages—is a brutal man in his youth. He loves God violently, and war, and small precious objects. He was reared in a bronze cradle; he is a man of the sword. He serves under Diarmait, and under God. Diarmait the king of Tara can count on his sword for raids in the Irish Sea, marauding cattle, crapulous feasts which turn into massacres. And God, King of this world and the next, can count on his sword to persuade the disciples of the monk Pelagius, who deny Grace, that Grace is devastating and can be weighed in iron. The small objects are also allies of God and the sword: they are won at sword point, and all of them—chalices, rings, or croziers—belong to God. The most beautiful, the rarest, the most precious—those that later, when they exist in plenty, the West will call books—speak of God, and God speaks in them. Columbkill prefers books to ciboria: for this military captain, whom Adamnan calls the Soldier of the Isles and of God, *Insulanus Dei miles*, this wolf is also a monk in the manner of monks at that time, a manner that is inconceivable to our way of understanding. When he lays down his sword, he rides from monastery to monastery, where he reads: he reads standing up, tensed, moving his lips and frowning, in the violent manner of those times, which we cannot conceive of either. Columbkill the Wolf is a brutal reader.

It is winter in the year 559, and he is reading.

He has just arrived at the monastery of Moville, built in dry stone on the bald heath facing the Irish Sea. It is raining the way it rains in Ireland; you can hear the sea below, but it is not visible. Finian the abbot has left him alone in the hut that serves as the library. There are four books: Columbkill leafs through the large altar copy of the Gospels, a copy of the *Georgics*, and Priscian's *Grammar*. The Gospels are a run-of-the-mill piece of work; he read the *Georgics* when he was in Cork. He also knows Priscian. He bends over the fourth volume: it is smaller and fits inside a little pouch with a strap that needs unfastening. He opens it at random, and reads, *I hate double-minded men, but I love Thy law.* He does not know this text. It is a great rhyming paean divided into a hundred and fifty smaller paeans. In the pictures on the facing pages you can see King David variously occupied with slaughter and music. The colors are very beautiful: an orpiment yellow and a vertiginous lapis lazuli. The blue and the paean are the book of Psalms. It is the first psalter he has ever held in his hand, perhaps the only one that exists in Ireland. He can hear the sea below dropping with all its weight. He sinks into the text.

For seven days he returns to the library and the rain doesn't cease. He reads standing up in his cloak, his hands numb with cold and his mouth voracious. On the seventh day he knows the text in detail: he has identified its articulations, he can recite the refrains; he has recognized the author's mannerisms, and he knows that what he holds in his hand is Saint Jerome's translation and that it was copied by the monk Faustus, because in the colophon he has read, *ora pro Fausto.* He prays for Faustus. He prays for Jerome. Despite Faustus and Jerome, a voracious sadness gnaws at his heart: he is going to have to leave the book behind. In the evening he dines with Finian and praises him for owning such a treasure. Finian beams with pride. Over Columbkill's wolfish face there passes a fox's smile. "Allow me," he says, to copy it. "I shall keep the copy for myself; no monastery in Ireland shall be able to boast that it shares Finian's treasure." Without replying Finian rises and leaves the table.

During the night, Columbkill slips from his bed. In the darkness of the rain and the loathsome thundering of the Irish Sea he reaches the library. Like a robber he lights a small candle and copies Faustus's text, which Faustus copied from Jerome. When he reaches Psalm IX, Finian enters and seizes the copy. The psalter falls, King David surrounded by blue plays his lyre. The wolf bares his teeth, but Finian is also a wolf. Both are sure of their right. Very calmly they set a date to meet at Tara in King Diarmait's palace, and he will decide which of their two rights is that of God. Columbkill is on his horse, which is streaming in the wet, and the rain and the dark carry him off *on the way that is dark and slippery,* as the psalm says.

At Tara, King Diarmait on his iron chair says, "The book

belongs to Finian as the calf belongs to the cow." Columbkill hurls his ring of allegiance at the king's feet.

All winter long on horseback he raises his warriors, forty decades of young men in Drumlane, twelve decades in Kells, thirty in Derry. At the feasts of alliance, when he is drunk and weary, he pictures the incalculable blue that seems to rise from David's harp. He is happy; he sings to himself the refrains from the psalms. In the spring all the O'Neills are under arms. He hurries to Moville with long day-marches and six hundred horse. Diarmait is waiting for him with a thousand horse in the bog of Culdreihmne beneath a clearing sky. Columbkill kneels down: he prays for Faustus, who is in heaven, the blue place which awaits us and favors us. He wants to laugh. He gets to his feet; they draw their swords. On the dark and slippery way they merge and set about each other; many young men are laid in the byre of death. At noon Diarmait lies in the marsh with a thousand horses, you cannot see them because it's raining much harder now, but you can hear them dying and you can hear the crows cawing with delight. Covered in blood and mire, laughing and drunk, Columbkill takes forty horses and gallops flatout to Moville. He can be heard laughing beneath the rain at the head of the cavalcade. When Finian opens the door of his monastery, he sees the other man halted there with forty warriors. Their cloaks are gray like the rain. Columbkill has a fox's smile and the eyes of a wolf; he holds out an open hand. Without a word Finian goes to fetch the little pouch and gives it to him. Forty horses sally forth beneath the dark sky.

In his war tent at Culdreihmne, Columbkill trembles as he
unfastens the little pouch and takes out the book. It is plump
and docile like a woman. It belongs to him as the calf belongs to
the cow, and a woman to her lover: it is his from the incipit to
the colophon. He wants to enjoy it slowly: he opens it, caresses
it, leafs through it, contemplates it—and suddenly he is no
longer trembling, he has stopped laughing, he is sad, he is cold;
he searches the text for something he has read and cannot find,
and the picture for something he has seen and which has van-
ished. He searches long and in vain, yet it was there when it
wasn't his. Everything seems to have been spoiled, to have
changed, and perhaps only the colophon is like itself—the colophon where the monk Faustus asks that people pray for him.
Columbkill lifts his head; he can hear the death throes of the
wounded and the crows' rejoicing. He steps out of his tent; it is
no longer raining, and above his head there are even large
patches of blue traveling over the byre of death. The book is not
in the book. Heaven is just an old blue place beneath which we
stand naked, and the things we possess are wanting. He throws
down the book, throws off his cloak and his sword. He takes the
habit, he takes to the sea, he seeks and he finds a desert in the
loathsome Irish Sea: on the bald island of Iona he sits down, free
and stripped of everything, beneath a sky which is sometimes
blue.

SUIBHNE'S LEVITY

The *Annals of the Four Masters* recounts that Suibhne, king of Kildare, has a taste for the things of this world. He is a simple man. Simple happiness and simple pleasures are his way. He is heavy and coarse, with nasty fair hair on his head like moss on a stone—and no delicacy of mind or soul. He wages war, he eats, he laughs, and for the rest he is like the brown bull of Cúailnge which covers fifty heifers a day. Fin Barr the abbot follows close behind this human monolith, and tries to remind him that the hereafter reckons even the thickness of a hair. The thickness of the soul is worse. Fin Barr lived for nine years at the tip of a headland, and nine more years on the lake, at Gougane Barra, with the seagulls and the crows: he is all mind and hands of glass. Curiously, he loves Suibhne because Suibhne is like a bull or a rock that might possibly have a soul. And Suibhne loves Fin Barr, who makes him feel, beyond the joys of this world, the joy of having a soul.

Fin Barr's brother is the king of Lismore. In the month of May, Suibhne takes up arms against the neighboring king. The pretext is unimportant: what Suibhne wants is the king's drinking cup, his fat cattle, and his wives. He also wants to stretch his legs and to ride his horse through the spring. He has sought the advice of Fin Barr, who said, "Kings go to war with one another, it's the rule. Make war on the king of Lismore since he's a king. But if you are victorious, spare my brother—who is your brother too, for are we not like brothers, you and I?" Suibhne is in excellent spirits, and he promises.

The weather is fine when they set out. They have bossed shields and polished scabbards. The army in the sunshine is like a gleaming stream. The war dogs chase butterflies. Suibhne sings at the top of his voice; his horse is thickset like him, and together they look like a hill with moss on the top. Fin Barr is also happy. There is blood beating in his hands of glass. He says to himself that in delight and contentment the thick soul of the king almost has delicacy and is at any rate clear; indeed, at that moment the king turns, looks round for him, sees him, and makes a very delicate sign with his hand. So, thinks Fin Barr, I shall save this soul—and if I save this one, the mountains too shall be saved.

The decades of the king of Lismore are deployed on the edge of the oak forests of Killarney. It's dawn, with the sweet breath of the woods. On the largest horse, in the midst of the handsomest warriors, with a crow's feather in his helmet, Suibhne can see the king, his equal. Suibhne himself wears a white feather, but the rest is the same. He's glad that the two kings are handsome. Above them there hangs a great silence, great expectancy, and the day breaking over the dew in May. The first cuckoo can be heard. Then it can no longer be heard, for Suibhne has raised his arm and his gesture unleashes a blast of thunder. All day

long, one step at a time, filled with happiness he moves closer to
the crow's feather. By five o'clock, the decades of both men are
scattered along the edge of the wood, and they are now face to
face: they look at each other, they laugh, they draw breath again
with a kind of roar. The wholesome frenzy of war that Suibhne
feels is suddenly mixed with another. The king with the black
feather is the image of his brother, slender and hard like him,
but with hands of iron instead of fragile glass: and this, strangely,
increases his frenzy ten times over. Before the other man, who is
still laughing, has raised his shield, he runs his body through
with his sword. He finishes him off with an ax.

Faced with the body his intoxication drains away. Suibhne's
soul returns to him.

The cuckoos call to one another through the forest.

In a clearing, the king sits on the moss, unlaced and groggy.
His head hangs down. He raises it. Fin Barr is standing in front
of him. Suibhne looks at him like a guilty child. For a long time
Fin Barr says nothing; then he curses him. And to finish he says,
"Your only brothers shall be the wolves in the depths of the
forest. You have no more soul than they." Fin Barr turns on his
heels, and Suibhne follows him like a dog. At the camp he sits
down on the ground, his head obstinately lowered, thinking.

In the evening, the soldiers round the fires suddenly see the
king get up and flee into the forest like a wolf. He does not
return.

Nine years pass. Fin Barr, the abbot of Kildare, is looking for
beams to fortify the abbey: in the oak forests of Killarney he

walks from bole to bole with his churls. They look upward, they compare, and they choose. In the fork of an oak tree that is too gnarled to be used as wood for making beams, Fin Barr sees, at the center of what he first took to be a tuft of mistletoe, a pair of laughing eyes which come to life and compose a face: it's a man, who raises his hand and makes a small, delicate gesture to the abbot. It's the king.

He leaps to the ground. He has a crow on his shoulder, which from time to time, when the king moves, flaps its wings a little and then very seriously smooths its feathers. Suibhne kisses Fin Barr; he laughs; he strokes him—but he cannot reply to his questions: he no longer has the use of words. Yet he seems to talk to his crow in a sort of jargon to which the other replies in the jargon of crows. And when the dialogue stops, the king sings softly, almost without pausing. He seems prodigiously happy and busy with his happy task. All day he follows Fin Barr and his churls, hopping along behind them like a crow himself. When they halt, he goes in search of berries and cress for them, and he devours it all with the same avid glee he had for the fare of kings, and the crow eats from his mouth. The churls are delighted. Fin Barr is moved; he strokes the ball of mistletoe and black feathers that was once a king. He says to himself that the king hasn't changed at all. In the evening he holds the large hand for a long time in his own long hand, lets it fall, and Suibhne hops away toward the woods, as if he were about to fly off. They will not see each other again before the bird of Death comes upon each of them.

The *Annals of the Four Masters* says that through the work-ings of Grace, King Suibhne has become a bird: that his feathers were given by the angels, that he catches the holy dove on the wing and speaks the divine word in the jargon of crows; that he is a saint and a madman, a thing of God. This is not entirely the opinion of Fin Barr, who returns to Kilmore in the melancholy evening on a cart that creaks beneath the weight of the un-dressed timber, his weary churls already asleep on the floor of the tumbril. Fin Barr doesn't know what to think. He is glad that Suibhne enjoys the state of sylvan tramp as much as that of king, that his joy is invincible and manifold like that of God. But he cannot decide whether it comes from the soul. A little woodcut-ter at the abbot's feet talks in his sleep, piteously, as if he were in distress. He is at the mercy of his soul. Is the soul what makes you moan in the dark? thinks Finbar. Or is it what makes you laugh and dance against all reason? My king, whom I cursed, embraced with passion the only joy that was within his grasp. Is this what it is to be a saint? Is it what it is to be a beast? Is it what it is to be at the mercy of the soul, or in thrall to the body? Only God knows, and the Four Masters, who have the ear of God.

Nine Passages on the Causses

BARTHÉLÉMY PRUNIÈRES

Barthélémy Prunières is on the Causse Méjan. He is looking for dead men. This is his passion. The fact that he is a doctor in Marjevols is of little importance: he prefers bodies that have ceased to suffer to the suffering bodies of his daily round. If at this very moment God or the devil were to appear before him on the causse and command him to justify his life, he would say, I am an anthropologist, a member of the Anthropological Society of Lille, the Anthropological Society of Paris, and the Anthropological Society of Bordeaux; in August 1870 I telegraphed my resignation to the Anthropological Society of Berlin. There is not a Society in Europe that does not know of me. I have shifted enormous quantities of ancient remains. I have studied Baumes-Chaudes Man, a fine dolichocephalic troglodyte who ate hare in huge dishes of unglazed clay, and it was I who named him. I studied Causse Man, the brachycephalus with the highly orthognatic face who belongs to the race I called *dolmenic*—it was I who named it. I had the honor of discovering that in both racial groups, the dolmenic as well as the troglodyte, individuals destined for the role of shaman underwent substantial trepanation in their early years; that a circular piece of bone the size of a five-franc silver coin was removed from their cranium; that this piece of bone removed from their head was worn round the neck as an amulet and made them all-powerful. To people who were disturbed by the barbarity of these practices, I said that gods who asked of man nothing more than a piece of his skull might be considered lenient. What the gods ask of me, each day, is to piece together the infinite puzzle of dead humanity.

He is on the Causse Méjan, at the southwest edge, just before the causse tips passionately down to the bed of the River Jonte, toward Saint-Pierre-les-Tripiés; he is on the site of the Cave of the Dead Man, which of course was named by him. It is autumn in 1871. The site is an ossuary in a rock shelter, which Prunières discovered in the spring of 1870; he dug it only once; he left little protection for it, thinking he would be back in a month or two. But war came, and with it the uhlans and sabers that perform excellent trepanations, and the gods who, when all is said and done, are lenient and will trade two years of famine for a brand-new republic. There have been two years of rain, frost, rodents, and landslips on the causse; when Prunières returns, half the ossuary has fallen into the gully.

It is autumn. Prunières has brought along Dr. Broca, president of the Anthropological Society of Paris (a man who knows us in his own particular way, though we do not know him: inside our skulls we each carry a cerebral convolution known as *Broca's area*). All day long they have assembled and named bones, like the gravedigger in *Hamlet*. They have placed them in two large crates that the curé of Saint-Pierre had carpentered for them. It's the end of the day. Broca is tired and stands smoking a cigar outside the cave; he looks at the autumn, the troglodyte bones in the curé's crate; he thinks about things and about the naming of things. Prunières is carrying out a final inspection of the gully before leaving. And there, three hundred meters farther down, he finds a very fine, very white humerus. At the same time as the bone, he finds the simple, beautiful sentence he will utter at the Bordeaux Anthropological Congress on September 12, 1872: "All the bones had been bleached white by the rain, the dew, and the snow."

In December 1893, Dr. Prunières is returning in the depths of night after attending a birth on the Aubrac plateau. He is caught in a snowstorm. He struggles on for several hours—he has a strong constitution, hardened by handling suffering bodies and bodies that have ceased to suffer. Then he gives up the struggle and settles himself between three rocks like an old troglodyte. He says to himself, "I am going to die." He repeats to himself, "Baumes-Chaudes Man, the troglodyte race, the dolmenic race, circular pieces of skull." He says to himself that his body will not be found. Aloud, he says, "All the bones had been bleached white by the rain, the dew, and the snow." The snow lays a maternal blanket over him.

He was still alive when he was found in the morning. He died during the day, from acute pulmonary edema.

SAINT HILÈRE

Bishop Hilère has abandoned his miter. His beard is quite white. He has handed in his crozier. He has founded a community of brothers no one knows where on the banks of the River Tarn, doubtless on the spot where Énimie, the saint with Merovech's blood, will later come.

Hilère is growing old. We know that he is growing old, but very little else is known about him. We know what he is not. He is not Hilary of Poitiers, who returned from beyond the grave to wield Clovis's sword against Alaric at the Battle of Vouillé. He is not Hilary of Carcassonne, who was there on the day of Pentecost, backstage with Saint Sernin, and who consequently saw the tiny flames above the heads of the apostles, observed the apostles twirling and humming beneath the fire like girls dancing in a ring, was convinced that it was the truth which danced and blazed like this, and followed Saint Sernin to the Gauls, a bishopric, and martyrdom. He is not the Hilary of Padua whom Correggio painted from memory. Nor is he Hilarion of Gaza, friend of Saint Anthony, about whom Flaubert brazenly said he was the devil. Our Hilère is also well acquainted with the devil.

He has made a little hermitage for himself, halfway between the Tarn below and the Causse Sauveterre above, on the edge of the cliff, in the locality of Les Baumes. It is flat like the palm of a hand. It combines the advantages of a chasm with those of a desert. You're in the dungeon of the universe, and yet on the top of the world: it's a good hermitage. This is where Hilère comes more and more often to escape the chatter of the brothers, to talk within himself to that other person who is God, and also to talk within himself to the other person he once was, when his beard was black. And here, in this very long conversation with himself, the devil will sometimes appear.

For whole days at a time, he takes the harmless form of naked girls. At other times, he takes the form of Hilère himself, wearing a tiara on the seat of Saint Peter. And at other times still, he has no form at all, just a light wind, beautiful sunshine, and the lovely fresh leaves on the poplars along the Tarn, a moment of elation, or a desire to stretch one's legs. "I'll climb up to the edge of the causse," says the hermit to himself.

It's very slow going, with endless detours. The old man has to keep stopping.

He is on the causse. The wind blows over it like the Holy Spirit. It is infinite but definable, like the name of God which can be woven into three Persons. It is the open palm of Creation, holding up to God a tiny blessed figure leaning on his stick. *The earth arose up by miracle by the will of Our Lord, in such wise that he sat as high as the other*: it's in the Scriptures and Hilère recalls it. He repeats the sentence to himself, and the wind blows over his heart. The wind plays with the trees. Perhaps it's the wind speaking to him: What need have you of a miter? What need have you of Rome? This is your bishop's seat. These are the seven hills, and God is directly overhead, with no one to stand between Hilère and Him. He is intoxicated with pride. He opens his arms, he runs, he's a little out of breath— and Lord, how the sun has sunk; he must get back before night. He turns away from the causse, the throne of Saint Peter, the bare back of the earth where nothing grows: he thinks he sees a little old monk leaning on a stick and laughing. It's only a juniper tree. "So it's you, Satan," he says reproachfully. He makes his way down as night falls. He can hear his miserly old man's breath in the night. Bats fly past; it's our own tiny heart beating up there. It's the tiny black heart of the pope, of Hilère, or of the lowliest cowherd. No one knows. One man is all men, one place all places, thinks Hilère. He wonders whether this thought comes from God or the devil.

ÉNIMIE

Énimie is the granddaughter of Fredegund, who had her rivals tied to horses' tails. She is the daughter of Clotaire II, king of Paris, who, for as long as his mother was alive, did not reign, and who has scarcely dared to reign since her death. Énimie is fifteen years old.

Clotaire is waging war against the king of Metz and the king of Austrasia. The king of Austrasia wants peace; Clotaire summons Gondevald, mayor of the palace of Paris, who can read and is on good terms with the mayor of the palace of Metz. They draft a treaty. On the first page there is a list of the possessions that the king of Metz will hand over to the king of Paris if he returns his weapons to their sheaths.

Clotaire is satisfied with the possessions that Gondevald reads out from the parchment. There are many distant priories among them, for which abbots must be appointed—fictitious abbots who will never set foot in them but who will receive the benefices. Clotaire accordingly makes himself abbot three times over, little Dagobert his son twice, Gondevald four times, and the remainder go to his close allies and cousins: Sigisbert, Gontran, and Caribert. The mayor and the king laugh, and drinks are brought. They pick up the list again and have a momentary hesitation because the next name is that of a monastery for girls, and as Fredegund is dead they are uncertain whom to allocate it to. The shade of Fredegund passes between them. They drink without pleasure—then Gondevald smiles: "Énimie," he says.

She is summoned. She is beautiful and pale, with jewelry made of hammered iron. She simpers at Gondevald. Gondevald looks at her bosom. He talks to her about a priory in the diocese of Mende, on a river called the Tarn, in a place with an unpronounceable name which Gondevald can nonetheless pronounce. He says to her, "You will be abbess of this place." He adds that it's a sort of game, that in any case she won't leave Paris or Soissons, that each winter she will simply receive sacks of gold from the distant place with the unpronounceable name. He tells her that of course all these sacks of gold will not really be for her, and that each year she must hand them over to her father. She looks at him. "Yes," she says. Her white hand places a little cross alongside Clotaire's little cross at the bottom of the treaty.

When she is alone, she wonders whether the Tarn is like the Seine, the Marne, and the River Oise. She decides that it isn't. She decides that this far-off place with the name which no one can pronounce should be ruled over by a young abbess and a mayor of the palace. She sleeps with Gondevald. When she unfastens her gown, she likes to think that she is offering Gondevald the abbess of an unpronounceable name. Her pleasure is felt in the body of an abbess. She asks her lover several times to repeat the beautiful pure Latin name, the name of her priory. He pronounces it with a laugh as he kisses her in the straw and the sheets. Then he stops pronouncing it. He is sleeping with Galswinthe.

She soon falls ill. It is said to be leprosy. When she dies at Soissons, she pronounces the unpronounceable name.

SIMON

Under the reign of Louis IV d'Outremer, son of Charles III—Charles the Simple— the Benedictine community of Saint-Chaffre becomes overpopulated and begins to swarm: a handful of monks settle in Burle, on the banks of the River Tarn, and restore the disused monastery which had been founded by a very ancient hermit. Having in their pocket a deed of cession signed by Pope Agapetus does not suffice: the barons in the valley do not like sharing privileges with the lords in monks' habits whom Heaven has visited upon them. The barons arrive with axes and horses; they make threats and steal a few chickens. Dalmatius, the Father Abbot, asks Brother Simon, who can read and use the noble tongue to perfection, to establish the legitimacy of the monastery in the noble tongue.

Simon ponders. He has the earth dug up beneath the choir of the old chapel, which has long since been ruined. Three skeletons, each holding a sword, are discovered, which he immediately has covered up again. Another is found, overlaid by the shreds of what was once a dalmatic and a stole. Simon ruminates at length over this one, and then after three days regretfully has it buried for a second time. A slighter skeleton is found whose dark black plaited hair has been well preserved and has gleams of life in it. It looks like a woman. "Yes," says Simon. He carefully cleans the hair and, one by one, the bones. He places them in a small wooden chest. He kisses the chest. He asks the carpenter brother to depict Our Lord on the Cross on one side of it and on the other a female saint.

He sends for Brother Palladius, who is young, likes walking, and is a passionate reader of the noble tongue. He shows him the wooden chest, where the carpenter has just started on the figure of Our Lord. He talks to him for a long time about an unknown female saint who is waiting with great patience in Paradise for two monks, Brother Simon and Brother Palladius, to restore justice to her in this world. He tells him that she appeared to Brother Simon in the form of plaited hair beneath the earth, and that she will appear to Brother Palladius in the form of a name in a monastery archive. It will perhaps be in the bishopric of Mende, perhaps in the bishopric of Le Puy; perhaps it will be at Saint-Denis, where the monks of the king of France live; or in Rome, where Our Lord is directly overhead. Brother Palladius must walk until the saint appears to him written in black on white. He will recognize her. Brother Palladius kisses the small wooden chest and sets out. Several winters pass: Brother Simon has time to read Athanasius, to reread him, to understand him, to copy the text, and to know the first three chapters from memory.

One spring he is sitting in the meadow, and he sees a vaguely familiar man coming down from the causse; from a certain way he has of cavorting as he walks, he recognizes Palladius. He gets up and makes broad gestures to him under the lovely clear sky. Up above, Palladius replies with both arms and starts to run. He shouts something that Simon can't understand, the same thing over and over again, like a name of three or four syllables which sounds like *alleluia*. When Palladius has almost reached the enclosure and shouts once more, Simon can hear the three syllables. "Enimia!" shouts Palladius. "So it's Enimia," says Simon.

So it's her. Enimia, the daughter of King Clotaire, sister of good King Dagobert, abbess of Burle in Gabali country in the year of Our Lord 610: this is what Palladius read when he visited the very learned monks of Saint-Denis—not a word more, but it's quite enough. Simon cuts his quills and prepares a fine calfskin parchment. He feels free, like a child, and yet serious, responsible for a dead woman as Our Lord is responsible for all mankind. For two weeks, every day when he rises he sees the well-stretched fresh parchment and the quills ready in his cell; he doesn't touch them, but he walks in the springtime. One day he hears a leper's rattle; he sees the leper walk past beneath the wide clear sky, and when he is close, it seems to Simon that the leper is a woman. "A princess sick with leprosy," he says to himself. He goes to drink from the spring at Burle. He says, "This water." Before his eyes, in the hollow of his palm like clear water, he has the entire life of the saint. He exults. He climbs up to the causse. A cloud hides the sun, the wind blows on the ailing trees. He doubts everything: the saint, the wooden chest, the name in writing at Saint-Denis. "Satan," he says. But he doesn't leave; he looks honestly at the open expanse. He kneels down, and he says, "Saint, don't let him stop you. Don't let him stop me."

He walks back down. In a single sitting, in the noble tongue, he writes the *Vita sancta Enimia*.

SANCTA ENIMIA

The anonymous monk who may have been called Simon wrote a *Life* which looks like this:

Enimia, daughter of Clotaire, is beautiful and pale. She is loved and desired by men. She thinks that she loves God, withdrawal from the world, silence. Her father the king wants to marry her to a ruffian baron by the name of Gondevald. She knows that she doesn't love Gondevald: he has an iron hand and hard, constantly shifting eyes which only come to rest on virgins. The wedding is set for tomorrow. It is night: the stable grooms are laughing in the courtyard, a few muffled thunderclaps can be heard in the distance, upsetting the horses, and in her chamber Enimia is praying, "Lord, do not let this man place his hand upon Thy servant." There is a louder clap of thunder, much closer by. It's night: the grooms have turned in and are asleep, the horses sleep standing up, the storm is a long way off. Enimia looks in despair through her window at the moon, and as she turns in the moonlight toward the mirror, which is next to the window, instead of her lovely face which men desire she sees a mask that is white and puffy like a wasps' nest. It's leprosy. Enimia bursts out laughing in the night. Prostrate, she gives

thanks to God for the excess of his goodness and his mercy. She
weeps and then sleeps.

Later, on another night, there appears at the window an ador-
able form which has come from the beyond. It's most assuredly
an angel. He tells her that the Lord does not want His servant to
remain leprous. That He loves His pale and beautiful brides.
That the wasps' nest that she bears on her shoulders is a trick to
get rid of Gondevald, and that she is now to be cured. "Drink,"
says the angel, "from the spring at Burle in Gabali country."
Something silken returns into the night, and Enimia can only
hear the Maytime nightingales.

The procession of the children of Merovech is now passing
through the gates of Paris and across the Berry, the Auvergne,
the great unknown territory—the oxen and the horses, the smell
of the byre, the hammered iron rings with enormous gem-
stones, the carts with crimson cushions and creaking wheels
whose axles bend and break, the barons, the royal retinue, the
bishops, the croziers, the ciboria, the grooms, and the little
veiled princess in the heaviest wagon. The slowness, the sea-
sons. Behind the hangings of the large wagon laughter can be
heard, and Enimia talking to God, to her goddaughter Galswinthe who laughs the most, and to her angel. God loves her,
and she will once again be beautiful; happiness is of this world.
The procession slowly crosses the causse, moves down the gash
made by the Tarn: the spring at Burle.

The hangings on the large wagon part; the princess steps

down. Her bare feet are made of white card like a wasps' nest. She kneels, she lifts her veil, she takes the cool water in her card-paper hand, she drinks passionately as if she were kissing her angel. For a long time her eyes remain closed, as if she were clasping her angel to herself, then she opens them and looks at her hand: it's the long, pale hand of a young girl. She throws off her veil and runs on her pink, young girl's feet. She dances and laughs till she cries. The barons, the bishops, and the grooms look at her. She looks at them with a sort of hunger.

Soon they are ready for the return journey. The hangings on the large wagon are open; the princess sits in it with her hammered-iron jewelry and her gown which reveals her arms and her shoulders, her universal hunger. Bishop Sigebert touches her arm as he talks to her, Duke Gontran her hair. She laughs loud and often. It is as if it were her angel touching her through each man. They set off before dawn; six pairs of oxen are placed between the shafts of the large wagon to climb the gash of the Tarn. When they are on the causse and they stop to unharness, it's daybreak. Enimia, who is looking at the daylight, wants to see it gleaming on her rings. She lowers her eyes to her hand: her rings are sunk in the puffy blisters of a wasps' nest. All her blood returns to her heart. As her blood stops, she says, "Satan." In front of her, Duke Gontran, who has seen nothing, is helping the grooms to unharness the oxen: the men's necks are thick, their hands mean on the withers of the oxen. She looks at her own hand again, and she says. "No, it is Thou, Lord." She draws the hangings. Behind the hangings, her voice very calmly gives the order to go back down.

She drinks once more, once again her feet are pink, and her hands are hands of love. But she doesn't throw off her veil. She will keep it on. She is beautiful for God—for no one, perhaps for nothing: to remember, to hope, to talk within herself to that other person who is the angel, to rejoice that she scarcely exists, to tremble, to be long in dying. Life is leprosy. The present hour is leprous. She founds, endows, and rules over Burle Abbey in Gabali country; she buries herself away there. She will never see Soissons again. When she dies, her angel carries her adorably away.

BERTRAN

Under the regency of Queen Blanche, around the time when Saint Louis is laying siege to the city of Damietta after setting out on crusade, Bertran de Marseille is bailiff to Guillaume, bishop of Mende, which means that he is the guardian of his seals and his writing desk. He is the steward of written things. He copies written things which prescribe the occurrence of real things between the bishop and the canons, the bishop and the villeins, the bishop and God. Nothing of what he writes causes real things to occur in the life of Bertran de Marseille. This suits him only in part: the flow of written words passes through his hands but does not belong to him, and he would love to divert it at some point, to dam it up, call it his own and be its master before God.

Bishop Guillaume notices his melancholy. And as he is merciful by virtue of his office, he decides to give Bertran mastery and something like suzerainty over a small piece of language. To do so he has recourse to a political pretext: the barons of Cénaret are again contesting the ownership of the spring at Burle by the monks of Sainte-Énimie; the barons of Cénaret are pettifoggers obsessed with legalities, but they have no education: they can neither read nor understand Latin. They haven't read the *Vita sancta Enimia* in which the spring at Burle is devolved upon the beyond. In order to nonsuit them, it will be necessary to write the *Life* in the vulgar tongue and, vulgarly put, to place all bets for the beyond on the spring. Guillaume knows that no one speaks Occitan better than Bertran: he was born and reared in Marseille—not the big, Greek Marseille, but the little Marseille that's a stone's throw from Volcégure, on the Causse Méjan. He was suckled on the obscure language of the barons.

The bishop rises at the hour of Matins. He walks through the outer ward and sees the dishes of lentils for the midday meal ready beneath the great crucifix in the refectory. He summons his bailiff to the audience chamber. Before him on the episcopal table there lies the very old manuscript whose parchment is cracking in several places: *Vita sancta Enimia*. The light from a candle falls across it. Bertran recognizes it at once: he has read it. Both men contemplate the antiquated object with a certain excitement. The bishop's hand caresses it and spreads it open. He says, "You will rewrite all this in the language that is spoken between Nabrigas and Saint-Pierre-les-Tripiés. The barons must be able to understand it. The jongleurs must be able to understand it and tell it to the villeins in the fairs. Even the villeins must be able to understand some glimmer of it, and laugh or shed tears when they hear it." Bertran, whose heart is pounding, says that he can do this. The bishop has rolled up the manuscript, and, gripping it tight in his hand, he uses it to emphasize each word as if it were a crozier: "What you write must be absolute like God's power, clear like the water at Burle, and visible like a tree or a dish of lentils. Make the absolute visible and clear. Describe to perfection a dish of lentils and the appetite you have for it; and without pausing to draw breath, use the same words to describe the appetite that God has for the spring at Burle. The barons do not doubt lentils, and they will not doubt God. They do not doubt the ownership of their porringers, and they will not doubt that God has his porringer at Burle." He adds, "For those boors to understand you, you will have to speak the truth and yet lie. I shall treat you as if you hadn't lied, but I cannot grant you absolution. Only the true things that you place at the heart of your lie can absolve you. You will be the master of it before God."

It is still dark when Bertran goes out. He is full of a taut joy like the bells for Matins. All winter and spring he is busy with written things that cause real things to occur between God and himself. Then he has finished. He brings the bishop a poem of two thousand lines in octosyllables and rhyming couplets written in the vulgar tongue: the *Life of Saint Énimie*.

It's summer. The bishop is sitting after dinner under the vine arbor at the bishop's palace, perhaps with a concubine. He is smiling and cheerful in the lovely light and the lovely shade. Bertran is very serious, intimidated, and proud, without a shadow of melancholy. He looks at his manuscript in the prelate's hands, between the strawberries and a carafe of ruby-red wine. "Did you put in the dish of lentils?" asks Guillaume maliciously. "Yes, Monseigneur," says Bertran. He becomes a little flustered and blushes: "And the strawberries too."

In the evening, when he is alone, the bishop reads. Yes, Bertran wasn't lying, the things he said are really there: the absolute and the visible, the absolute is hidden but clear at the heart of the visible. There is the Causse Méjan, sin, and salvation. There are the names of the places; each bend in the Tarn is named; each stone along the Tarn appears as it is itself, and not the one next to it; and behind the stones, the Drac monster and the saint—which is to say Good and Evil—appear, disappear, and confront each other: Good and Evil hurl themselves at stones that can be named. There are the many forms taken by the created world, which is to say the visible stakes over which Good and Evil do battle. There are miracles, ramrod stiff corpses that supplely rise up and walk, rocks that climb the gash of the Tarn of their own accord, trees that speak unaided of God's power, which is to say absolute Good applied without contradiction to visible form. There is the doubt that grips you when you cross the causse and it's raining, which is to say Evil. There is a woman who disrobes three times and whom we see three times naked in the spring at Burle—but this lovely body in which Satan with all his might has laid his trap is a body that is true and pure like the hand of God: the inconceivable and nonetheless visible body of a saint. Good is the utterly naked body of a young girl.

The bishop looks black on white at the naked body of the saint. He has an appetite for the forbidden flesh of a saint. God is in this flesh. He rejoices and weeps as will the villeins in the fairs, when the jongleurs recount the *Life of Saint Énimie*.

SEGUIN

Seguin de Badefol has just taken Mende.

He no longer knows where he was born. Ever since he was able to speak he has sold his body, his horse, his glove, and his sword: he's a captain. He has fought under King John with the Fleur de Lys. He has fought under the Black Prince; last September at Poitiers with the Black Prince they captured King John beneath an oak tree in the gully of Maupertuis. The Black Prince has returned to Brittany, King John is under lock and key in the Tower of London—there are no more princes to pay for employment in war. No matter, others can become princes; after you've had truck with them and been under their heel you learn what a prince is: a man with fur-lined cloaks worn over iron who grinds villeins in his mill and makes excellent flour out of them. So it is that the somber barons of the Great Companies, whom the English call warlords, have flourished and wield power.

For ten years—or five—Seguin has excelled in the iniquitous business of being a prince. He keeps a tight grip on the bandit princes who rule thanks to the vacancy of King John. He has called them by name. He has shouted their names in combat. He has traded a horse or a parish with them, insulted them,

loved and hated them, betrayed them, ridden with them, iron
boot against iron boot, at the hour in winter when, as evening
comes, they have nothing to say to each other; he has dismounted and drunk with them. They have been drunk together
on air, on wine, and on blood. He has ridden and dismounted
with Bertugat d'Albret, Petit-Meschin, Perrin Boïas, the Bastard
of Armagnac, Guyot du Pin; with Arnaud, known as the Archpriest; and at other times, with complete indifference, he has
fought them when they took it into their heads to grind villeins
that Seguin himself was planning to grind. He has fought the
entire world. The armor is heavier in the evening. The ermine
looks gray when night falls. Seguin is growing old; he abandons
the fat lands of Burgundy and Berry to the Archpriest and the
Bastard of Armagnac; he settles on poorer, less coveted lands
where the villeins endlessly bow beneath the rain, the famine,
and the warlords. He has his fief in the Limousin, and from
there he has the Limousin, the Gévaudan, the Rouergue, and
the Auvergne revolve at his behest, the way you make a top spin
with a whip. He wearies of this occupation. He has white hairs
in his beard, which he is apparently the only one to see: no one
has mentioned them to him.

He has just táken Mende with Perrin Boïas and Petit-Meschin
under his command, and they have seen the white hairs in his
beard quite distinctly. They find it hard to put up with the
suzerainty of the old man. All day long they have killed, seized
plate, girls, and fur-lined cloaks. All night they have drunk,
among the huge, swift flames made by the peasants' huts, and

the slower, richer flames made by the wooden structures of the burghers' houses; and suddenly it is daylight: the flames grow pale and the sky appears. It's a gray sky. They are full of gab and wine. They feel like ghosts, airy flames, gods or devils, the way you feel in the sleeplessness of early morning. One of them—a young fellow—suggests setting off straight away to see if there is a monastery willing to open up or to burn, if the peasants' women are in the right mood, if the devil is around. They're up like ghosts. They kick the valets awake, and they are laced into their battle dress. Their fur-lined cloaks over the top. In the saddle. Iron boot against iron boot, five or six captains and men-at-arms. And now they are on the Causse de Sauveterre, galloping along, full of dismal wine with the dismal sky above their heads. The sun has not once appeared. The open expanse is arid, like a captain's life. There are trees growing here whose names are known only in Purgatory. It is the open palm of the earth offering up five or six captains to God or the devil. Seguin de Badefol pulls on his reins and halts. His face is ashen, like his beard. "I'll not go any farther," he says. Perrin Boïas and Petit-Meschin exchange a glance. The horses have stopped on the causse. The dull mist of the clouds blows against their armor. Strangely, Seguin, in an ashen voice, starts to speak—of God, of what it is permitted to do on earth and what it is permitted not to do—and he might well speak of remorse if he had the habit, the use, or even the memory of the word. Perrin Boïas and Petit-Meschin smile. The first man touches the hilt of his sword. He says, "Old men go no farther than this." Seguin is silent: he looks for a moment at the open expanse, the stunted trees, the interminable horizon. Perrin Boïas does not have time to draw his sword fully from its scabbard before Seguin slits his throat. Seguin sighs. He wipes his blade on the mane of his horse. The horses' breath creates soft little clouds at regular intervals. He heads full tilt toward Sauveterre. "Let's keep going," he says.

ANTOINE PERSEGOL

On June 9, 1793, under the rule of the one and indivisible republic, the Montagnards have swept away the Girondists, the Commune rules, Robespierre rules, *compassionate zeal toward the unfortunate* rules, and Antoine Persegol is walking on the Causse de Sauveterre. He is walking in the company of twenty-one lads from La Malène and some others, from Saint-Chély and Laval—forty-seven in all. They have weapons and they are drunk: they were plied with drink down in La Malène to incite them to join the troops of the *True Friends of the Monarchy*, the army led by Charrier who was *député* for Mende and is now a Chouan. It wasn't difficult to persuade them: they are peasants or carders, weavers paid by the piece; poverty is their lot; and the great upheavals, the foreign wars, and the Law of the Maximum have made their poverty twice as bad. Down in the town an hour ago in front of the pitchers of wine, it was child's play to get them to blame the republic for the grim poverty that only recently they blamed on the king.

Antoine Persegol is walking over the Causse de Sauveterre with his scythe on his shoulder fashioned into a pike, the tip of the blade in the longer part of the handle. Others have bayonets. They all have the white cockade. The open air has sobered him up a little, and he is very uneasy: he is secretly fond of the republic. He thinks about the republic the way he thinks about his mother, who has stayed behind down in La Malène and wept when he left: something old and frail yet constantly fresh, that always needs him. He thinks that the republic has occasionally asked his opinion, like his mother when she is preparing dinner and asks him whether he would prefer broad beans or lentils. He thinks that the republic regards him exactly the same way it regards Baptiste Flourou, even though he is the lowliest of the carders and Baptiste Flourou owns twenty carders, all the wool that they card, and the mills where they card it: the republic regards both of them the way his mother regards him and his brother André, who has been an imbecile since birth.

The wine is wickeder. It is absolute like the king. Wine made him take the white cockade and put his scythe together back to front.

They reach La Capelle. They enter the village. From each house, from behind each stone wall, and from under each tree there emerge the blue uniforms with the red trimmings of the one and indivisible republic. It's the Bleus. They have cavalry. They have a superintendent with a tricolor sash who gives orders in the language that is spoken in Paris. The forty-seven men surrender without a fight: the wine has drained away, abandoned them in the June sunshine, and without the wine they suspect that the republic is not the only cause of grim poverty. Antoine Persegol feels as if a great burden has been lifted from him.

They are parked in a small sloping field with stone walls. The roll is called, then they are left for a while, with a Bleu posted at every second stone along the wall. They do not speak. Antoine Persegol tells himself that everything will be straightened out, since the republic loves the truth, and the truth is that he loves the republic. Truth is the mother of freedom. The truth will appear, and this evening he'll be free; he'll see his mother. He can see the superintendent with the sash walking to and fro beneath the elm tree on the square, a lad his own age with worn hands like those of the carders. He looks like a decent fellow. He loves the unfortunate, that's for sure. Antoine Persegol walks up to the wall to get a better view of him: he'll signal to him and the other man will come over; he'll talk to him, and they will patiently allow the truth to emerge between them, lovely and indubitable like the tricolor silk. A Bleu roughly pushes him away; he goes back and sits down. Toward evening, carts arrive. As they are being led away he finds himself by chance in front of the superintendent. He says in patois that he'd been drunk and that he loves the republic. "What's this scoundrel saying?" asks the superintendent in the language that is spoken in Paris. The sergeant shrugs his shoulders, and the superintendent turns away. They are loaded into carts and taken to Florac. So now he will explain everything in Florac, and he'll see his mother tomorrow.

The reality is otherwise. Reality is a cruel stepmother. The next morning at Florac five men sitting in black hats speak in an incomprehensible language to forty-seven men standing before them. They are pushed into the June day with their hands tied. On the cart he thinks about his mother standing in the June day on the doorstep of her house in La Malène, looking toward the far end of the empty track. The huge machine with the swift bevel is set up on the square in Florac. Forty-seven times the iron blade of Mother Death severs a head from a trunk, forty-seven times a head severed from a trunk violently confirms the law of falling bodies. Antoine Persegol is the fortieth.

ÉDOUARD MARTEL

At Le Rozier on the River Tarn and the River Jonte, where the three major causses meet—Sauveterre, Méjan, and Noir—Édouard Martel is sitting on the terrace of the Hôtel des Voyageurs. It's September. He is in his prime; he's about to succeed in life, and he knows it: that is what he is telling himself on this sunny terrace in September, between the vast sky above and the sparkling waters below. He proudly contemplates September. He holds his head high with its fine Roman features and blond goatee. He is one of those men who love glory. He has abandoned the sad profession of scribe at the court of law in Paris; it seemed to him that for a man of his caliber the profession of explorer was the shortest path to glory; it also seemed to him that the surface of the earth, the ground on which you walk beneath the sun, was too easy a terrain for the explorer's quest, too obvious and somehow duplicitous: he has taken the darker part of exploration, the caves and the chasms, Erebus and Tartarus, the kingdom of the dead. Within this kingdom he is searching for his own, like Dante or Orpheus. He has founded speleology. A hundred feet below ground he has created a reputation for himself.

He loves the causse where this reputation originated when

he discovered Dargilan ten years back. He is looking for other holes. He has made the Hôtel des Voyageurs his headquarters, like his African colleagues, the discoverers in pith helmets, who pitch their tents in Timbuktu or Zanzibar and from there gather information about the desert in the North, the forest in the West, send out patrols and wait for the dry season. The shepherds from the causse know the man with the blond goatee who has a liking for the Underworld, and sits with his legs crossed under the arbor on the terrace waiting for them to bring him news of the Underworld: if the earth opens up under a lamb, or if a stone dropped down a shaft is swallowed up without a sound, they come running to the Hôtel des Voyageurs and talk to the blond goatee with the crossed legs clad in gaiters. And on this very day, September 18, a man who has news of the Underworld is walking into the village of Le Rozier.

It's Louis Armand, the locksmith. He is now under the arbor. He is full of a feverish joy. He says that on the causse between Nabrigas and La Parade there is a low entrance; the stones thrown into it drop the devil of a way down. "Well then, let's go to the devil," says the blond goatee with a laugh. As soon as he has been up to his room and fetched ropes, pegs, carabiners, helmets, and lamps they're off.

Until the end of September the terrace is deserted. Or it seems that way because, although are there are a few drinkers in the afternoon—shepherds or carders, and a few passing horse dealers—the tall blond figure whom glory has brushed with its wing and who gives meaning to other men is no longer there.

Autumn reigns alone; Martel does not see it. He is beneath the earth; he is exploring, mapping and measuring the most enormous hole he has ever seen. A hundred feet below ground he is tasting pure happiness.

In October, Martel, now somewhat paler, is sitting under the arbor. It's a beautiful day again, and very hot. There are pens and an inkpot on the table, a blotter, and several sheets of paper which flutter in the wind like the leaves on the hornbeam above his head. All morning Martel has been lining up figures, calculating contour lines; he has sketched cross-sections, scale drawings; he has made a portrait of the chasm: the first hole, the enormous sloping nave with its stalagmites, the second hole lower down which is like a duplicate chasm. He contemplates the drawings with a sense of vertigo. Suddenly he lifts his head: the hotel owner's wife is serving aperitifs to the short-stay guests and looking tenderly at the proud profile and the blond goatee. She doesn't know that Édouard Martel wants to die. She doesn't know that he is saying to himself, "None of this has the slightest meaning. It's just a hole that slopes. These are just white stones rising up in the dark. The sun has never been here. It's sinister. There's nothing to see inside." He stands up angrily, crumpling his papers as he takes them away. In the evening he gets drunk with Louis Armand. The hotel owner's wife tenderly helps him upstairs to his room.

Later, on another day, he is once again under the arbor, which is at present quite bare. He has just been to the telegraph office, where he sent a cable to Paris, and he is now sitting down.

He is calmer. At the top of the sheet that caused his despair the other day—the one with the scale drawings—he has carefully written in capital letters: *Aven Armand,* and under it in smaller letters: *At La Parade Causse Méjan Lozère.* He says to himself that it's a good start. By the spot where the stalagmites are particularly bushy and numerous, he writes *Great Forest;* he immediately crosses this out and writes *Virgin Forest,* and then where they are all round and heaped on top of each other, *The Jellyfish Corner.* He goes through them, one by one, and against this or that stalagmite, he writes, *The Grand Stalagmite (30 m), The Easter Candle, The Palm Tree, The Turkey, The Tiger.* He can see very clearly in his mind's eye the tall shapes as they appeared to him down below. He smiles: No, these are not white stones rising up pointlessly in the dark; they are objects full of meaning that have a name in men's mouths. As he is making these observations to himself, the telegraph clerk arrives bringing him a reply from Paris. He reads it and exults. Without lifting his pen from the page, he writes under the drawings, *The whole of Notre-Dame in Paris could be comfortably contained inside the large chamber.* He rereads his words and tastes pure happiness. He says to himself that the profession of scribe is a fine one. He strokes his blond goatee.

ABBOTS

FOR AGNÈS CASTIGLIONE

I

It is to some secondhand chronicles, to the *General Statistics of the Vendée* published in Fontenay-le-Comte in 1844, and to a belated happenstance in my own life that I owe the tale I am about to relate.

It is the year 976. Ancient Gaul is a hotchpotch of names bolted to lands, which are themselves names: Normandy belongs to Guillaume, Guillaume Long-Sword; Poitou belongs to Guillaume, Guillaume Towhead; France belongs to Eudes, duke of France; the crown, that trinket, belongs to Lothaire, the king, which is to say squire of Beauvais and Laon. For Anjou and the Marches it's Robert the Calf and Hugues the Abbot. Alain of the Twisted Beard controls Brittany. And the diocese of Limoges is in the hands and under the miter of Èble, brother of Guillaume, not the Long-Sword but the fair-haired, frizzled Towhead. The towhead has two characteristics: it is too fair and too full; it blazes up in an instant. Guillaume is too fair and his anger gallops like fire. Èble has his brother's towhead but without the tow's two qualities: beneath the miter of the one and the helmet of the other you can see the same hirsute swirl of frosted locks, the same frothing fuzz, the same crushed straw with short curls, but on Èble's head the tow does not catch fire at the least impediment; on Guillaume's head it does.

Whether Èble's towhead might blaze for other reasons, this tale will tell.

Èble has spent his life putting out the fire on Guillaume's head: he has kept watch on the embers, cultivated the ash. The real policies of his brother—the alliances and the gifts, the endless parleys—were carried out by him while the other hothead drove his flames against Long-Sword, against Eudes, against Alain, against anything that bore a name and a lance. Èble is weary; he's thrown in his hand and withdrawn from the world. He is sixty years old. He has relinquished the bishopric of Limoges and the monastic benefices from Jumièges, Angély, and Grammont. He will never again have the pleasure of excommunicating anyone. He no longer has the power of the keys, the power to condemn paltry or wicked souls to hell, nor has he the patience to run his cool hand over the boiling head of Guillaume. Fire is no longer his affair. On the midget island of Saint-Michel, facing the vast sea, he is contemplating the clouds and the water. For he has kept the midget Abbey of Saint-Michel.

The monastery is devoid of charm, thrown together with planks of wood and peat, for the whole thing, which was founded and consecrated by Philibert the Ancient, has been trampled a hundred times over by the Normans—burned down, bailed out, rebuilt, taken apart. The walls of the chapter house are cob, the cloister is raw brick. The choir is older, built of the local white stone, but the fires have turned it black. It is fire too which melted the great bells, and the ones hammered by the blacksmith brother are small and shrill. A ring of logs forms the library—which, besides some canonical odds and ends, contains the *Life of Saint Martin*, the *Life of Saint Jerome*, and much learned bullshit from before the Revelation. Right up against the library is the very long, two-story hut where the monks eat and sleep. All these buildings have landed here like dice thrown from a cup. The eye meets nothing that has been made to last. It's named for the wilderness, the hermitage, Saint-Michel-en-l'Herm. It suits Èble very well. He has merely fortified the islet with good white stone from Luçon brought by water on barges, so that people can tell from afar that this hut belongs to God, which is to say to Èble the abbot, who has the gift of quelling fire, even the fire belched by a Viking dragon. Èble is the man of unimpressive stature and bulk, but with a completely white and remarkable towhead, who is contemplating the water in the month of May around the year 1000.

The water does not consist entirely of water.

The midget island sits just inside the mouth, facing the sea where two rivers marry, the Lay to the right and the Sèvre to the left: and as it happens these nuptials are rich with sand, mud, oyster shells, and all the debris that rivers calmly snatch up and crush: windfall and dead cows; the waste that men throw out in sport, from necessity, or from weariness; and sometimes their own human bodies thrown likewise in sport, from necessity, or from weariness. With the result that it's neither the forthright sea nor the honest river that Èble has before his eyes but something mixed and tangled: a thousand arms of fresh water, as many arms of salt water, and as many again of water that is neither fresh nor salt embrace a thousand plots of naked blue mud, naked pink and gray mud, red-brown mud, worthless sand where the devil—which is to say nothing—plies his trade. Besides, he is the only being able to set foot here because everything else—men, dogs and horses, field mice—is instantly swallowed up in a shroud of stinking gases. Only the flat-bottomed barges come this way bringing the monks' pittance over the water's arms, and even then the water is so thin that you need to use long poles to sail across the mud. It's not earth, because seagulls screech above the eels, or sea, since crows and kites fly up with vipers in their beaks. Èble is not sure that this does suit him so well: it's like when you don't know whether the meadow at Longeville belongs to Twisted Beard, Long-Sword, or Towhead, and you have to unsheathe iron and square the parleys in order to decide whether Longeville belongs to one of the three or to all three at once, which is as good as to say to the devil. Èble thinks for a moment about his brother Guillaume, softens at the memory of this man of fire who doesn't belong to the devil. He pictures Guillaume with broigne, halberd, and helmet, his fair tow hair in the wind, lance held aloft, riding his horse determinedly across the marsh, flying over it at an angelic gallop, like Saint George. Èble smiles, though you can't see it since we're looking from some way off and his back is turned as he leans against the fortifications, a tiny dark figure bearing a radiant head at one end—for this is a black monk, a Benedictine, clearly silhouetted and visible against the white limestone.

This same evening in May, after Vespers and None, at the hour when the first lamps are lit and before the first psalms are sung, he summons all the monks to the chapter house: some fifteen patricians like himself, drawn or banished here by a violent reading of the *Life of Saint Martin*, by their courage, by their cowardice, by a brother who wants to rule alone because the fiefdom is only small, and—who knows?—some by God. A few lay brothers too, clerks of humble origin, called by the prospect of bed and board, and some by a desire for books. You can hear the seagulls and the sounds of water. Èble looks at them one after the other in the early lamplight as it dances on their faces, faces that are sharp, heavy, crushed, burning, or calm. Then he makes the sign of salvation, and the others do the same, casting huge shadows of arms onto the cob walls. He allows more silence to go by—he knows how you govern, he has parleyed in close-fought argument with Louis, late king of France, with Alain and Eudes; he has even taken fiefdoms with a smile and a few pretty words from Guillaume Long-Sword, a Viking's son and almost a Viking himself—he lets them contemplate at leisure his towhead and his mouth, from which there will emerge a sound that is different from the cry of the seagulls which measures time. Eventually he asks Brother Hugues, who is young and a clerk, to come and stand beside him and to open the Book.

He asks him to read the Third Day of Creation.

Hugues's voice is strong and young, crushed and burning. He reads, "And God said, Let the waters under the heaven be gathered together unto one place, and let the dry land appear: and it was so. And God called the dry land Earth; and the gathering together of the waters called He Seas: and God saw that it was good. And the evening and the morning were the third day." Hugues trembles slightly. Èble stretches an arm toward the window which gives onto the mouth of the river, and he says, "We have reached the Second Day. The earth and the waters are not disentangled. We shall make the Chaos and the Void which lie beneath into something on which we can set foot. Saint George must be able to ride his horse across it and cows graze upon it. In a year from now I want to plant my crozier on it and have it stand firm without being swallowed up by the great maws below." The gulls are heard again. Then the psalms are sung.

■

The next day before dawn they take the two barges that belong to the abbey, launch them on the trickle of water, and set off in search of the arms that will separate the Chaos from the Void. Abbot Èble is part of the expedition, and Hugues is there too. Each of them is sitting in a barge, two acolytes with poles in each stern. They know a little about the arms they're going in search of, as these are the ones that fish for themselves and for the monks, and live on the little islands nearby, Grues, La Dive,

La Dune, Champagné, Elle, Triaize. From one barge to the other in the backwater, they joke about these natives who stink of fish. They say that they worship rain like a wandering idol. They say that they piously coat the crosses which are planted for them with honey, and make them offerings of bird carcasses and flat stones. They grant that they are tall and often handsome, with arms of iron, for the miasmas from the marshes carry off so many in their early years that those who survive are made of iron. They grant that they are gentle. The monks visit them from time to time and talk of salvation, the natives listen obligingly but barely understand the language. However, they understand perfectly when the monks say to them: so many barrels of herring to the monastery for Christmas, so many thornback skate and carp for Easter, so many sardines for the monks' everyday fare. It's because they're half fish, says Hugues. But we still christened them, says Èble. They laugh, and the huge pale sky above the two tiny black monks laughs too, along with the gulls.

They disembark at Grues, at La Dive, at Triaize. There are huts with drying fish, one or two ambling cows. They gather the fishermen or their womenfolk, whatever is to be had: faces that are sharp or heavy, crushed or burning, assorted bodies dressed in tunics which look very like the monks' cowls, except that they are not necessarily black. The monks make the sign of salvation over them and they all sit down. The monks tell them that they are going to drain the marsh at the foot of Saint-Michel, transform mud into rock, work a miracle. Ever since the monks spoke to them of miracles, they have retained the word, and they listen more attentively. The miracle requires their arms. The monks tell them that this miracle land and the cattle it will bear are to be shared, half for them and half for the monks. The monks say to them that those who are enticed by this prospect should follow them at once, and set up their shacks in the meadow by the monastery for several months each year over the summer—and that they will be able to return to their homes from October to mid-May, when the marsh reverts to being forthright sea and honest river. It is Hugues who does the explaining in his beautiful, burning voice, and Èble adds that besides the extra land and the cattle they will have salvation. The natives talk for a long time among themselves; some go back to their nets, but others don't. On Dive two couples with their children launch a barge and follow the monks; on Grues a silent old man and two young men; on Triaize no one. They land on Champagné.

It's the middle of the day. They are hungry.

Six black monks climb the steps of the harbor on Champagné, and they are now in the middle of a ring of huts. On Champagné the men are hungry, too; they have all returned from fishing and raised the nets and the creels; fish is cooking on the huge fires. The explanations, the hires, and salvation can wait until later: six black monks sit scattered among the fishermen, talking of sturgeon, pike, and the summer months. They laugh; the steaming bowls are filled. Èble has not engaged in talk and is sitting alone; he is tired, irritated with himself; he is wondering what possessed him yesterday to tangle with watercourses—what pride, what diabolical imposture. Someone hands him a bowl; he looks up. Above him a very young and beautiful, very serious woman is holding it out to him with an open hand. She has a strong nose and lips, wide open eyes. She is tall and her skin is white. Her bare feet are like marble. Èble blazes in an instant.

Èble is indeed the brother of Towhead, and it's time to say so. He too can burn. It's true that his fire doesn't take the form of a shimmering hulk that gallops about with halberd, broigne, assorted ironware, and a lance at its tip; his fire is more subtle, less noisy—his two fires, that is. For he has retained the two passions which come from the fire and which smolder assiduously beneath the black hood in the hut at Saint-Michel, as they smoldered beneath the gold miter at Saint-Martial in Limoges, amid the fumes from the incense: his two flaming torch brands, glory and female flesh. Glory, which is the gift of spreading fire within the memory of men, and flesh, which has the gift of consuming bodies at will in a spike of flame or a bolt of lightning. And the tall woman who is standing in front of him, and who is already walking away on her feet of marble, has the unbound vertical force of a lightning flash.

Night is falling; the huge twilight sky is red. After Champagné, the six men in black set up their bait of cattle and salvation on Chaillé, Île-d'Elle, La Dune, Le Gué, and they land a good catch. More than thirty barges are following them, laden with many arms, men, women, children, and a few gray cows. In one of these barges there is the woman from Champagné,

with her husband the fisherman. Èble looks at her, and he sees
that Hugues is looking at her. She is looking at the water.

■

May is drawing to a close.

In the library they have the books that speak of the land and
the sea, like the two verses from the Third Day but with less
solemnity: those by the captains who always need to drain a
little water for twenty legions to keep their feet dry as they pass
with catapults and horses (Caesar and Constantius); those by
the historians who recount how the towheaded tyrants set about
putting a mountain in the place of a lake, a torrent in the place
of a mountain (Cassius Dio and Tacitus); those by the dabblers
and the agronomists (Pliny, those who wrote to him, and those
who refuted him); and Augustine, who proves that matter and
miracles are joined like mortise and tenon. They all pore over
these books, argue fiercely, make plans, decide on the equip-
ment needed, and share out the tasks. Èble does not take part
and is bored. He thinks fondly about the ragings of his brother,
who is fully armed and already in the saddle, setting off at a
gallop, and whom he couldn't restrain. He can't restrain himself, either. He opens the door of the library. It's a morning of
fine May drizzle. He pulls his hood down over his head. He is
now in the meadow where the gentle savages who believe in
cattle and salvation have set up home. They have built huts out
of the beeches that grow here and, under the direction of the lay

brothers, a forge and a carpentry shop. The gray cows wander here and there beneath the drizzle; the black abbot with his hood goes straight to a hut he knows. She is squatting on her feet of marble. She's alone; her husband is at the forge. He throws back his hood; she sees the towhead. She bares herself up to the waist, she lies down, she opens. He looks at the wound of wet fire in her tuft of tow, then sees it no longer because he has plunged into the fire. She cries out like a seagull, the bolt of blue lightning unites them; beneath his hood Èble returns to the library. He passes Hugues, who is walking toward the huts beneath his hood.

Sometimes with exasperation, at other times with enjoyment, but always with pride because the glory will redound to him, Èble follows the summer's work from higher up. He sits on the fortifications, his legs dangling over the marsh, or else he stands and makes the sign of salvation over all the bustle. He can see that the brothers have indeed read their Pliny or their Augustine, unless they are thinking of Moses when he parted the waters or are just adapting their hands marvelously to the decrees of their minds. Their method is simple. Starting from the edge of the little island the natives mark out a plot of two or three acres; they surround it with planks of wood so that a man can touch bottom. From this wooden deck the natives dig a deep ditch and pile up the earth to form an embankment; inside the plot, the women and children dig another ditch against the embankment, building it up further, stamping it down, beating it, making it firm. Èble loves to see the two feet of marble beating the mud, the same feet which each day beat the empty air in pleasure, raised and cleansed by the bolt of blue lightning. After two weeks it is possible to walk without fear on the plot, in three it is dry. By September four plots have been disentangled from the waters. Laughing, praying, rejoicing, Èble puts on his abbot's miter and comes down to plant his crozier. It remains upright, it stands in earth. Fifteen male voices sing out, the natives kneel.

In the evening, when the husband has gone to put out the creels, when wordlessly she bares herself from feet to waist, the fire is wetter and burns hotter: she has seen the miter, she has seen the crozier, and it is the miter and the crozier that she has behind her closed eyes, between her raised feet. The bolt that shatters her is a man's member but the glory is of an abbot. Èble sleeps content; he dreams that the little thuribulers from the past in Limoges, God's little dancers with their dancing dishes, the incense for the bishop, the breath of God are huge, utterly naked women.

The rest are working twice as hard. The monks have decided on large, very heavy plows, with long broad plowshares, for six oxen and four men: they need to dig deep, beneath the lighter pink and gray surface silt, the green, to reach the blue silt beneath which is fat and heavy, and then to mix these different colors together. And for these huge plows the furnace in the forge never goes out, either by night or by day; the iron is beaten at nighttime, dipped red-hot into water, where it cries out, wedded with tremendous force to great pieces of oak to form the plowshares, and the fresh young oak burns and shrieks. Each night before Compline, Èble goes outside, walks to the hut or not, depending on whether the husband is away fishing or not, but each night he sits in the meadow to enjoy the orgies of sparks, the loud cries emitted by the iron as it submits. He thinks about his brother. He thinks about the love that his brother had for iron when it is mastered to the point where it molds itself to a man's body as closely as wool, or when it is allowed its ferrous freedom, when you thrust it through the body of another man and it emerges dripping on the other side. This kind of iron is glory; it's like the silk on a miter and the gold on a crozier. He lifts his head; the stars tell of another glory—the gold and the iron of God which stamp the dark night. Once, when he is absorbed in this heavenly reverie, Hugues soundlessly sits down nearby and looks at him. The sheaves of sparks light up the tow of his hair here and there, turning it to gold. Hugues passionately wants to kiss the tow, and also to rip it off. Èble leaves the stars, sees Hugues sitting there. Hugues has told him in confession that he too makes the feet of marble rise from the ground. He loves Hugues, who knows the books and reads them in a throbbing voice; and he would also like to thrust thirty inches of iron through Hugues's young body. For a long while they remain silent, each thinking to himself about the two feet raised above the other man. The shriek from a wheel of fresh wood being strangled in a ring of red-hot iron by the cartwright soothes them both. They talk about the blacksmith brother who is a colossus, about his violent character which is nonetheless contained, about the rule of Saint Benedict beneath which monks groan but are purified and hardened, like iron in the furnace. Hugues observes that the rule speaks of gold, not iron. And that it is in gold that glory is visible, not iron. Èble remains silent for a long time, then he suddenly asks Hugues what glory is. He asks if it's power. If it's a name that echoes for centuries in the memory of men. If it's for God alone, brilliant and brief, like the blue lightning bolt in the hut, or interminable and lost in the air, like reading, or like singing. If it's fixed like the stars, or wayward like the sparks. If it's pure. He asks if it can be mixed— with matter, with ambition, with the body of a living man. He asks derisively if draining twenty acres of land taken from the Chaos and the Void is glory. He falls silent. Hugues does not pause to reflect; he's a young clerk with hollow cheeks who throbs, who knows, and who wants. He says, "Matthew says that Jesus says, *Ye are the light of the world. Neither do men light a candle, and put it under a bushel, but on a candlestick; and it giveth light unto all that are in the house. Let your light so shine before men."* He adds that glory is good and honest like gold; it's flagrant and visible; it's a miter, it's fire, it's the cloak of Saint Martin—and all this must be shown to men. It's ten acres of land reclaimed from the marsh because a mitered man willed it, because twenty men in black and fifty fishermen created it. He hesitates; he looks away from the abbot and says in a less confident voice that the devil can make use of glory, that it was glory he showed to Jesus when he took him to the mountain. Then they hear movement between the dormitory and the choir; they get up, they go to sing the Vigil. Èble thinks about David, about Bathsheba, about Uriah the Hittite.

∎

At the end of September, Èble blesses the plows. There's no time to lose; the rains are coming. Ten gigantic plows, ten war machines with handles as long as a lance and as broad as a thigh, and six oxen fettered, two by two, to the shaft. Èble is croziered and mitered in the early dawn. He can see them from above on the new land, like ten catapults erect and pointing at Saint-Michel. He walks down; he makes the sign of salvation over these diabolical machines and the horned herd. All at once the men shout, the oxen move off, and the machines follow; the earth opens; red and black are mixed: one monk by the shaft, four fishermen taking turns and propped along the handles. At the due hour the monks climb back up the little island and go to sing; the natives guide the oxen and maintain the furrow on their own. The chants fall like dew from above onto the sweat and the shouting, the panicked muzzles of the oxen, the earth that is shifted and laid bare. The fishermen eventually know the chants, take them up down below. The children run and dance along the plowshares, day after day.

One morning before Lauds, as the autumn drizzle is setting in and the plowing is coming to an end, an equipage arrives on two barges, with men-at-arms and an imposing figure who seems to be wearing a squirrel-fur hood, but it's hard to be sure:

day has scarcely broken. The lookout brother goes to fetch the
abbot, and leaning against the outer wall beneath their black
hoods the two men scrutinize and speculate, say that it must be
this person, or rather that. The barges dock, the imposing figure
stands up in an agile movement, and the moment he sets foot
on the first step the abbot recognizes him: it's Benoît, who was
like a son to Èble in the days of incense and the purple ring, and
whom he named coadjutor at Saint-Hilaire in Poitiers. Today
he's the one who wears the purple ring on his finger. He has
come in person. He's taller than Èble. Beneath the squirrel fur
he looks a little like Hugues, but his skin is not as dark, his
cheeks not as hollow. On the terrace in the drizzle he kisses the
abbot's hands, they embrace, and he says, "Your brother Guillaume is dead, and before he passed away he asked us to convey
his farewells to you." No, he did not die by iron; he too was tired,
he'd thrown in his hand, he drew his last breath at the monastery
of Saint-Cyprien, surrounded by orisons. They embrace once
more, black hood alongside gray hood they walk to and fro,
Benoît talks about the departed warrior, about the other men of
fire: Foulque who now controls Anjou, little Hugues Capet who
controls France and whose teeth are long. Èble isn't really listening to these tales of secular matters which no longer concern
him; his thoughts are wandering. He looks at little Benoît who
served mass for him and who wears the purple ring; he thinks
about Hugues, who is the same age as Benoît, about the sons he
never had, and about the iron Guillaume used to brandish at
every turn: when he was drunk, when he was joshing, when he

was choked with anger. He weeps for Guillaume from the bottom of his heart, but there is something in his tears that gladdens him like wine. The sun is fully up now. The fishermen are walking down to the reclaimed plots with the oxen. Together they look at the war machines that require twenty arms to lift the shaft and yoke the oxen. Benoît remarks that the oxen in the third team are exhausted, and the lead ox is jerking its head the way they do when they're about to turn nasty. The bishop retires to sleep, the abbot in the chapter house distributes the tasks for the day. For the shaft of the third team he picks Hugues.

The drizzle persists all morning. The animals have gaiters of mud right up their legs, as heavy as they. Around noon, an ox on the right-hand side of the third team collapses, and on the left-hand side the lead ox, exasperated by this resistance, bellows and charges. Hugues, who jumped to the wrong side, the left, takes the charge full in the chest; he falls, five standing oxen and one slumped ox trample across his body, and finally thirteen inches of iron slice his body in two.

It's the first death since the monastery has been restored. A hole has been dug in the old cemetery, which dates from the time of Philibert—a few bones from the time of Philibert have briefly seen the light of day again. Hugues arrives in the white shroud; the monks have piously washed and anointed what remained and disentangled the bones from the mud. They have placed a plank of wood inside the shroud so that the two pieces look like one. The sun has returned. He is laid in the earth; his beautiful throbbing voice will never again be heard. The shrill bells all ring out, the beautiful confident voices all sing, and, deep inside, each voice hears the voice that throbbed and is dead. Bishop Benoît without miter or cowl sings among them as if he were one of them. Then the seagulls can be heard: Èble slowly steps forward without miter or hood, pronounces the prayer of absolution for the dead. The vast red twilight shines through the white towhead; he looks like a saint.

The fishermen on the barges leave to set up the nets for the night catch.

Next to the bishop at the guest table, the abbot's place is empty. He is not seen either at Compline.

He has been walking in the old cemetery where Hugues's fresh cross is all there is. Once the barges have left, he is inside the hut. A body, or the earth in its entirety, bares itself up to the waist in the dark. In the dark a plow slices a man in two, a man-at-arms expires in a slow death agony, a brother kills his fellow brothers. The world is gathered in a wound of wet fire, and this world can be joined and then disjoined at will. Shifted thus the world cries out and exults. The abbot cries out and exults. He returns to the cemetery, where the moon has risen. He prays for Hugues before the tiny new cross, he laughs and weeps, and once again he hurries to the hut. He leaves only when he hears the voices of the fishermen. As he leaves, he passes the husband on the doorstep. For a moment they look at each other in the moonlight, then each goes where he must.

He wakes the bishop. Benoît lights the little oil lamp, puts on his stole, makes the sign of salvation over the other man, sits and listens while Èble kneels and speaks. He painstakingly confesses what he knows. He weeps frequently; he talks about Hugues's throbbing voice, about Guillaume whom he loved, about pleasure, and about the things you don't want to share. When he is finished the bishop absolves him with the customary penances. He tells him that the flesh is evil, which they both know, and that it is the lesser evil. He tells him that the lead ox on the third team is not called Èble; it is one of God's creatures and endowed with freedom. He tells him that the first blood to be spilled consecrates a piece of land. He tells him that glory—the glory of having expanded Saint-Martial in Limoges, of having established fiefdoms on the fires lit by his brother, of having restored to God a hundred acres of land reclaimed from the Chaos and the Void—has already overlaid his infamy with gold, just as the glebe will tomorrow overlay the blood of Hugues. He tells him to rise; he kisses his hands.

In the middle of October, when the fishermen are piled into the barges with their cattle and their children to return to their islands, the woman is pregnant. As she leaves she very quickly kisses the abbot's hand; she smiles at him.

■

All winter long the monks maintain the ditches and fortify the embankment. The reclaimed land remains as land on which the rains trickle down without eroding it. In the spring there is grass growing on it. The monks beam with delight and cavort about on it; they speak of miracles and agronomy. Èble laughs too. Saint George gallops in the meadow; a woman awaits him behind a dragon. The cattle are put out to graze on it. When the days lengthen in May, the barges arrive with their freight of rain worshipers who have come to serve God. Some have died or are occupied elsewhere, but there is a greater number of new arms. The woman from Champagné is not there.

Nor does she return in the following summers. The monks reclaim a hundred acres each season, and now after the plowings on the oldest land-takes they are growing beans and corn. The place where Hugues died remains a meadow, and Èble thinks he sees that in the spot where blood was spilled the grass is thicker. The twilights are vast and red, or sink, modest and damp, in the drizzle. The monks now have great deep bells which have come by water from Limoges, engraved around the rim: *Benoît, bishop, to Èble, abbot.* Storms sometimes pass overhead, the blue lightning bolt shatters the great raised arms of the plows. None of this is of concern anymore to Èble. He spends hours just sitting, in the chapter house or the cloister, on the grass in the meadow. He leaves the prior to take on the business of allocating the tasks, of being proud of successes, or of weeping over failures. The towhead fades, memory grows weary, it can no longer disentangle Hugues from Benoît, or Guillaume, or Denis who arrived two or three years ago and whose throbbing voice drowns out the others. It can no longer disentangle the woman of the marshes from the viscountess of Chalus, Adélaïde, or Mathilde, who were once avid and penitent, all of them pierced by the lightning bolt, stripped bare, marked by a wound and by cries. All these figures join hands and dance before him, couple and kill each other, embrace. All things are mutable and close to uncertain. Sometimes he gives a solitary and mostly cheerful little laugh: he is thinking about glory, and that draining lands is like blessing crowds with the purple ring. It is undoubtedly glory, but all these things are very precarious candles which are quickly covered by the bushel and then lit elsewhere. The red twilight does not move; everyone knows where it is lit without changing, and at the root of this unchanging glory there is no man, living or dead. Èble is on good terms with the death that is on its way; it is written into the round of life, and it is not glorious.

He walks down to the harbor. It's the dead season of Christmas, when the fishermen bring barrels of herring and the finest fish—sturgeon and pike—for the table at Epiphany. The winter morning will be very blue; it's already blue, but a few patches of mist are still traveling across the water. Out of the mist, heading straight toward him, a flat-bottomed boat emerges in which plump fish gleam. In the prow of the boat there stands a small, fair-skinned girl with a head of tow, a thousand densely packed sunbeams, gold that shines against the silver of the pikes. She bears the torch of daybreak. The sun exists for this brilliance, the blue belongs to her. It looks like a crown. It looks like something else which Èble knows well and which is not himself or his brother Guillaume. The abbot thinks very quickly, and what comes to mind is the word *glory*.

The little waves slap against the boat, the seagulls make their usual complaint about the world, the word *glory* is borne directly to Èble.

The boat docks; in the stern with his pole he recognizes the man from Champagné. The little girl jumps onto land, very quickly kisses the abbot's hand as she has been told, picks up the big fish and throws them into the baskets. What brilliance. Her tiny bare feet are firmly planted on the white stone. The gold straw covers her eyes, and sometimes a little hand impatiently pushes her hair aside. The abbot and the man look at each other, like the other time. His beard is turning gray now, and he looks like Saint Joseph. "Is this your daughter?" says the abbot. The man replies with a resolute Yes, and that they have had three other children since. The baskets are full; the little girl leaps like a flame; she is in the boat, in the mist, the blue completely envelops a black monk among the baskets of sturgeon.

Sometime later—weeks or years—he senses that he is dying. He summons the monks, requests his stole and his crozier for the kiss of farewell. The monks fetch them; they bend over him and talk of the God who awaits him, in joy, in glory. Yes, Èble who can no longer see their faces sees that glory does exist, and that it is manifest. That glory is a mixed thing. That it is a dazzling flame which burns bright when it encounters things that are mixed. This he accepts. It is born of the women's wound, it's a fair-haired little girl who appears, sparkles, and vanishes. For Guillaume it was mixed with iron and with blood. For God it's mixed with the choir of angels and the actions of men; it's mixed with the flesh of the Son who bled on the Cross. It's mixed too with the embroidered stole which has been placed on him and with the crozier which he grips with a withered hand that shakes. One by one the monks bend down and give him the kiss of farewell; for one last time, shaking as he does so, he makes the sign of salvation over them. He lies back in the glory of the chant for the dying sung by thirty virile voices.

The boat arrives. The monks see him sit up with a start and cry out; he's afraid he might see two sections of a dead man. But there's nothing except a small, fair-haired girl. He climbs aboard, and she ferries him away.

II

It is to Pierre de Maillezais, who was certainly not called Pierre but chose this monastic Christian name when he renounced the world, who acquired the name Maillezais neither from his place of birth nor from his family but as a monk in the abbey of Saint-Pierre de Maillezais, and who wrote his *Chronicle of Maillezais* in the years when, from the kennels in Hastings, Guillaume, grandson of Guillaume Long-Sword, was releasing his hordes across England—in sum, to this hybrid, this forgery, this purely nominal entity that I owe the tale I am about to tell.

Pierre relates that in the beginning, long before he was a monk, even before he was born and the monastery existed, there was a boar.

Guillaume, son of Guillaume Towhead, observes this boar. Night after night, he waits and watches for it with passionate attention. Not that there is any shortage of boars: he puts up three a day, or more; he lets them run, this not being the season for boar. Surrounded by water, Maillezais is a deep oak forest where the acorns fall like manna on the population of wild pigs which groan and grumble beneath the shelter of the trees. But this particular boar seems determined, is enormous and enigmatic. Its coat is gray and at the withers it stands taller than a mastiff. Guillaume is watching the edge of the wood at twilight; he doesn't wait long: the beast's head appears, its forequarters emerge from the wood, it snuffs the wind with its snout, and Guillaume has plenty of time to see the huge, barely curved tusks, like daggers. Then it bolts and reappears a little farther off, or a little nearer by. It is requesting, tempting, willing. When day comes, no beater has put it up. Pierre in his *Chronicle* is undecided as to whether the boar is a demon or an angel, or at any rate a messenger.

Guillaume has reached the end of summer with a great fanfare, accompanied by his constable, his household, ninety-four companions and sergeants, his birds, and his blue hounds. It's just a forest surrounded by a beach and rocks, with not a living soul. Since his father's day there has been a hunting lodge on the tip of the island, wooden turrets above the water and the forest, pallets for the knights and the horsemen, and, right in the middle of it all, the reason for the existence of the turrets, the pallets, and the stables: a vast covered hall for banqueting. Guillaume—Guillaume Fierabras—is young and powerful, he is free, he has just succeeded his father, and he is disporting himself with tracking game, dancing, and wine. He's happy. He has also brought the women with him, and Emma, whom he took in Blois and married yesterday in this very spot: she disports herself with tracking game, dancing, and pleasure. She is happy. He loves her flesh. She has a curious way of observing Fierabras, sidelong, with the smile that is special to dark-haired women who have a good head on their shoulders.

She too observes the boar.

Around the Feast of the Holy Cross in September the men and the blue hounds are busy with hart; the women hunt hare on the shore with hawks and sheld-fowl with slender, quivering dogs from Syria. The gray boar emerges from the russet oak wood, and twenty paces off he trots the length of the procession, as if he were following them. The few Syrian dogs foolish enough to approach him are gored without causing him to even swerve from his path. The women turn back and retreat to the castle; they set up a gallop, the boar gallops too, twenty paces off; they take fright, but not Emma. She has a sort of fondness for this monster: it's like night in full day, like a horse that has scented wild cat and quivers beneath her, like Fierabras who quivers on top of her in the night. He doesn't leave them until they reach the postern; he trots unhurriedly back toward the tree cover.

At the Feast of Saint Andrew in winter, when the oak woods are smarting in the frost, Guillaume decides that from today they will hunt boar; he's had enough of hart and buck or wolves. The varlets remove the green tunics worn for deer, put on the gray tunics with which you kill wild pig. The knights have ermine and wolfskins, and they make a fine picture. They are carrying spears and the special four-foot-long swords, whose blade has no cutting edge on the knuckle-bow side. The cavalcade, the ermine and the gray tunics, the blue hounds calmly reach the tree cover, watched by the women in the turrets. Emma in her furs remains on the turret; until the last minute she looks at the wolfskins on Guillaume's shoulders, the wolves' heads tossed back and dancing against his hips. There is only the water on the shore and the breeze in the oaks, and then suddenly a great galloping. In the forest you no longer hear the *Ho moy, ho moy! Cy va, cy va!* of the hart, but the *Avant, maistre! Avant! Or sa, sa!* We're in the Middle Ages, of course, horses' breath in winter, codified cries in the depths of the woods, blue frost.

Ten days, and four times as many boar have been taken, but they haven't seen the gray. The women, however, have seen him on the edge of the wood as usual, snuffing the wind, and once he even came as far as the postern, within arrow's reach. Guillaume is now infuriated; he wants this animal, he'll have it. He will not have it.

At this point Pierre's *Chronicle* introduces a character who serves the workings of Providence: it's Gaucelin, whose body, says Pierre, is sturdy and bright, and I cannot tell whether this brightness is valor, a fair complexion, good looks, or the soul made visible. He has not been conjured out of nowhere, and I will add to Pierre's *Chronicle* that he is a very young man, an apprentice knight, a squire from the House of Blois. He has not yet fully attained chivalry: he still sleeps with the churls and sits at the lower end of the table. One evening, as the slender crescent of the moon is appearing just above the woods and the men are finally returning through the archway with their pig carcasses, their enormous hunger, and their laughter, the gray boar thrusts his forequarters between the trunks of two oak trees; he allows his whole body to emerge, takes a few steps so that he can be clearly seen, and waits. Gaucelin has lingered—for a call of nature or from a tendency to daydream, given that bright souls like to linger in the bright frost beneath the moon—he is still in the saddle on the shore. He sees the beast and immediately swings round; he races toward it alone with three blue hounds which had also dawdled. The boar doesn't move. The other ninety-three men are unharnessing; they've not seen or heard a thing in their loud laughter. The women have seen—Emma's heart beats in her throat. Gaucelin is right over the beast: he can hear its breath with its thick hide and tough bristles, and in the very instant that he hears it, the breath, the hide, and the tough bristles plunge into the forest at a gallop. Providence, the sturdy bright body, and its three blue hounds disappear after it.

The women hear the furious gallop through the dead leaves and the specific cry, then nothing more until, after a time which seems astonishingly short to them, Gaucelin sounds the capture loud and clear.

Emma is the first in the saddle, with two churls carrying torches. The trail is easy to follow—they had charged straight ahead. There at the top of a nearby hill, in the light of the torches, two lifeless hounds and a horse are swimming in blood and their own entrails, a single blue hound licking its wounds to one side. Gaucelin is lying against the dead head of the boar, whose withers are pierced by twenty inches of spear, its hind-quarters still inside the wallow from which it had confronted its pursuer: they have dismounted, the torches dance along the ground, the wallow is a very ancient construction crudely built by human hands—a dolmen no doubt. Emma kneels over the squire; he opens his eyes, sees the small dulled eyes staring through the tough bristles and above them Emma's laughing eyes, and above them again the horn of the moon. He strokes the coarse bristles, and with his other hand still gripping the calling horn he strokes Emma's face. She throws her ermine over him. The horsemen arrive, the hounds. Guillaume embraces Gaucelin at length. Emma is on her feet again and stands facing them all. She is radiant.

She says it's a sign from the beyond. That perhaps the dead boar was an angel and so is flying around them in the dark. That it was perhaps a demon which wanted to have done—a demon's lot is hard, even when gorged with acorns beneath a thick hide. That Gaucelin, who died before her eyes, has come back to life, as the torchbearers can testify, and they flamboyantly testify. She says that the ancient construction is the altar from the old priory of Saint Pient, Saint Pient the hermit their grandparents used to talk about. That the boar is perhaps also Saint Pient, the untamed part of Saint Pient, the part of the soul which is hackled with tough bristles and tusks, which stirs and grunts inside each of us, even hermits, the part of Saint Pient which was waiting in Limbo to be set free and dispatched this sign to them each evening. She says they must inform the men of God and with their permission rebuild the monastery. She asks Guillaume for sole control of the monastery. Guillaume hesitates, then agrees.

They are all filled with zeal, their hearts beating; it's good, after the hunt, to hear a woman talking determinedly about

God. The consecrated candles are fetched and arranged around the dolmen or, rather, the altar, and on the altar itself. Huge fires are lit. The boar has been dragged a little farther off, a stick placed in its open jaws according to custom. Its head and feet are cut off. It is speared from one end through to the other so that the bristles can be singed above the fire, the hide scraped. The blue hounds sit with their tongues hanging out, and wait. Meanwhile, Guillaume kneels before the altar in his wolfskins and prays, Gaucelin kneeling in Emma's ermine prays, and Emma prays, standing behind them without her fur-lined cloak; she isn't cold, she's burning. This nuptial island between two rivers, the bed of her pleasure, will no longer just be this hulla-baloo where ninety-four men halloo and blow horns, it will be the chanting of eighty black monks held in the palm of a hand that belongs to a tiny, dark-haired woman. She will rule over the island like Guillaume over Poitiers. Blessèd be this boar. It's the *curée* now; the boar is disemboweled, the paunch and the guts are thrown on a bed of embers, pink bubbles burst in the black blood, the swollen blue entrails scream like water in fire: for in those days it was believed that the flesh of the boar should be cooked even for the hounds. They whine quietly, and finally they are thrown the smoking innards on the tips of pikes; they pounce on the food. The carcass has been skinned; the hide is hanging on a branch in the frost close to the moon; the choicest pieces are being roasted for the men. The sergeants and the squires have been sent away—only the flower of chivalry has been kept to enjoy the flesh that has been touched by Providence, fewer than twenty mouths—and Gaucelin, who has joined them. Wine has been brought up. They eat like wolves, and between two wolf mouthfuls Gaucelin looks at Emma. She asks that with Gaucelin's consent, since it's his by capture, the boar's hide be reserved for her. Gaucelin joyfully consents.

■

In the lay chapter of Saint-Hilaire and in the chapter at Ligugé owned by the black monks, Emma's request is considered. It has on it the seal and the coat of arms of the House of Poitou. The scribes are consulted: Yes, Saint Pient did go into the wilderness, the oldest chronicle in Ligugé certainly mentions his dilapidated hermitage, but it is on the reverse side of a leafy initial; the copper oxide in the green has eaten away both the initial and what was behind it so that you can't read clearly whether it was at Maillé, Maillezais, or Chaillé. It is to be Maillezais. Theodelin, a monk at Ligugé and a very young one, comments that a boar does not constitute proof and that Martin of Braga said as much: "Many demons preside over the forest." They scoff at his timidity and point out to him that the House of Poitiers controls Aquitaine and half of Anjou, and that it was the countess of Poitiers in person who saw the hand of God on the boar. The abbot takes Theodelin in his arms and draws him to one side: he tells him that the order needs another foothold in the bay and the marshlands, the first foothold having been established at the far end by Èble of Saint-Michel, many years before. Theodelin is the son of converted Jews, and he takes the point. The black monks inform the mother house, Cluny; the request is accepted, then ratified by the chapter and the bishop of Poitiers.

In the spring Cluny sends the abbot, Gaubert, and the rest are levied from Ligugé and Marmoutier: a contingent of thirty young and hardy monks, including Theodelin. The horsemen vacated the site in March for war, against Brittany or Anjou, or perhaps both—they haven't yet decided. Only Emma, who saw Providence, and Gaucelin, the arm of Providence, have stayed behind to guard the altar, along with Emma's women and a few of Gaucelin's companions to guard the two of them, to plunge hawks' talons into the backs of hares, and to banquet. They are all at the harbor to welcome the monks. Gaubert is lordly, suave, and inflexible; he steps down from the boat like a pope, presents lavish compliments to the House of Poitiers, and sees only the House of Poitiers in the tiny woman but not the joyousness or the fire. Theodelin, the small swarthy monk, can see them. He sees the tall bright squire who is the same age as him, and beneath this brightness the fire. They walk up the hill—the path is now as broad as an avenue—beneath the oaks which are greening up. Instead of fur-lined cloaks, there are velvets and woolen cloth, crimsons and azures, pearl grays, all dancing against the fantastical Benedictine black. Up at the top they sing. The monastery, says Gaubert, will be dedicated to Saint Peter, the patron saint of Cluny. Saint Peter—Pierre—will rule over Emma's nuptial bed.

Cluny is powerful: the architects and the stonemasons, the image makers, are hard at work within a week. The yokels drawn from round about are clearing the land; the barges with their blocks of white stone each as tall as a man—one block per barge—pitch and sometimes capsize; they never stop, two hundred blocks of stone per day. On one occasion a boat turns turtle before Emma's eyes: there's a great splash of water, then endless stinking bubbles, the entrails of the earth, as two tons of white stone drop right down to the bottom of the mud with the passion of falling things. No matter. Emma sees the raising of the nuptial bed, its whiteness, its strength, all of it arranged around the black altar, the old wallow, which has simply been faced with stone and whited. The image makers have carved two large overlapping birds on the capitals that look as though they are pecking at two smaller birds beneath them. Gaubert hunts with hawks; he shows that Cluny, the salt of the earth, already has a foothold up in heaven, and is busy with birds; he has delegated to Theodelin the illusory power of raising buildings here below. Theodelin dreamily listens to the wind in the oaks; he thinks about the demons who preside in the forests, and that God is being installed in their place. He wonders whether his brandnew power comes from the demons or from the cunning of Cluny, which can transform demons into white stone or sonorous coin. He gets along well with the tiny woman who loves power; he accepts her advice. The architects say whether a thing is possible or not, create it or not. If it turns out as she wanted, a capital or a door, she discovers and savors the meaning of the words *power, hope.*

Gaucelin has other hopes. He recalls the moment when after

the terror, after the thick breath and the enormous tusks a hair's breadth away from his belly, he caressed the life being restored to him as it bent down under the blade of the moon. The *Chronicle*, as we know, says that his body is sturdy and bright. The arm of Providence brushes Emma's arm, the tall bright young man seeks her hand, grasps her by the waist in dark recesses and tries to embrace her; he follows Emma and Theodelin as they walk together round the building site, and, amid the white stone that is being raised, he sees only the crimson skirts, the bare arms. She firmly eludes him. She loves Gaucelin too; he was her Providence, but Providence is not made of flesh. Emma does not want to mix one thing with another: she is for Guillaume, who is making war and for whom she is waiting. She is not irritated by Gaucelin's desire, or if she is, it's with a certain delight, and sometimes she's on the point of yielding. She doesn't yield. She has the boar's hide tanned: it's been hemmed and chamoized, but it remains rough. She wears it belted beneath her gown against her skin, as if, in his absence, to feel the rough hand of Guillaume upon her. Guillaume has taken Angoulême. He'll be coming with his wolfskins. The summer is over. He's here.

This year there are a hundred and twelve of them. Guillaume climbs the hillock, embraces Theodelin and Gaucelin but not Gaubert, who has left to spend the winter at Cluny in the saltworks. Theodelin shows him around, explains. The construction of the choir is complete, and when Guillaume sees the altar he doesn't recognize the wallow, the winter's night, now covered in a canopy of white linen, the gold cupboard which contains the coin, the sacred vessel. When he is told, he bursts out laughing. Emma looks at him with her sidelong little smile; it's her own body that he's exploring and laughing over or praising, it's across her body that his spurs ring out. She belongs to him the way the choir here belongs to Christ. The others are already sounding their horns; they are after the hart; Gaucelin and Guillaume go after it too.

Thirty nights or more of nuptial revelry. When Guillaume saw the leather pulled tight against bare flesh under the gown, the delicate skin flayed around her waist, he too began to burn. The hunt continues through the night; he tracks and he finds, he allows his quarry to escape, draws it in, and takes it. They bounce up and down, then collapse—and no, these are not the grotesque postures that the monks in Cluny say they are, the frantic gestures of the damned, but the precise and perfect gestures of the mort and the capture. Emma sounds her own capture and sounds it well. Her body is here and sounds the horn, and it's also out there built in white stone that shimmers beneath the moon, where large birds peck smaller birds, and the monks chant. When he embraces her in the evening she can hear Compline, when he takes her at daybreak it's Matins. Life is an unending chant.

At the first moon of winter, the gray tunics and the wolfskins are out again, the *Avant, maistre! Or sa!* the boar. The maistre returns in the evening, slung from the pummel by the feet, dripping. Gaucelin excels: he brings back more than all the others; he wants her to see that this debauch of gashed hides and blood-soaked bristles is for her. The others are envious. One evening, Hugues, one of Gaucelin's companions who stayed behind all winter and who eats at the lower end of the table, lashes out at Gaucelin, who had dealt the death blow to a wild pig that Hugues himself had surprised in its lair. Everyone has drunk a lot; they are laughing, then they stop: Hugues says that it's not just the animals put up by others that Gaucelin is adept at taking; he's equally adept with the women that others have flushed out. He names the countess. Guillaume asks her to rise and come and stand before him. She is very erect and pale; she denies it. Gaucelin says nothing. Guillaume banishes him. He's in the saddle beneath the moon, heading for the court in Anjou.

The count does not repudiate Emma because the House of Blois is strong and holds the House of Anjou in its pincers, or perhaps it's for other reasons. But he no longer looks at her.

Until Christmas, Emma sleeps alone; she hears the Vigil and Matins, she wears the tight pig's hide day and night, she thinks about her power, and she keeps up her hope.

∎

Pierre, who doesn't linger over these amorous annulments or the hunt, reports that in the depths of this second winter the powers gather at Maillezais to draw up the charters, declare what the abbey is, under which rule, and what it shall be. Pierre indulgently describes the powers gathered here beneath the hand of God, through the happenstance of a boar. The boats bring purple and crimson, scarlet beneath the wolfskins: the men stepping down from the boats look across the swaying oak wood at the spire rising tall and straight above the choir. The archbishop of Bordeaux looks, the bishop of Saint-Hilaire, the bishop of Saint-Martial, and the bishop of Saint-Front. Gaubert looks too; all in black and more fantastical, he has dragged himself away from Cluny to come to this place and represent the suave and implacable salt of the earth. And the great vassals, their wives. They all of them draft and hunt. It's the High Middle Ages, with its beautiful images, assiduous scribes, and horses.

I am tired of these images, tired of Pierre's bland *Chronicle*. The rest goes quickly: you have only to look at the viscountess of Thouars, her fair complexion and her bursts of laughter, her tall figure, her brightness, like Gaucelin if Gaucelin were a woman. She smiles with passion at everyone. Her sturdy bright arms can control a horse like a man. She follows the men going after boar, she likes their company. She rides alongside Guillaume, their eyes mingle, he takes her. It is she who each night now sounds her own capture in the count's bed. Emma can hear.

What follows is scabrous and romancical. Pierre, who relates it without blandness, retreats prudently behind his sources: his master the learned Arcère and the *Gallia christiana*, and the tale that Theodelin told him in person. One day, as the prelates and the men-at-arms are reading the charters to one another, arguing every inch of the way for a meadow or a tree, the women go hunting with birds of prey—but not all of them: it seems that

Ermengarde de Thouars is alone with Emma, Emma's falconer, and Emma's varlets, who have kept the Syrian dogs on a leash. They are hunting with large birds, goshawk or gyrfalcon, the ones that kill buck, in the glades close to the abbey where Emma wants to steer them. She looks sidelong at the passionate smile when the birds of prey plummet. Suddenly she seizes Ermengarde's saddle by the pummel, strikes her across the face with her crop, and unseats her. Ermengarde has understood and is already off at a run. The falconer and the varlets have stopped. "She's yours," says Emma, and they release the dogs and the bird, they run. Ermengarde flees toward the abbey; she's almost there, the gray tunics hot on her tail, the Syrian dogs nipping at her heels, the gyrfalcon seeking out her eyes. She collapses; they all take a lengthy turn at her beneath the walls of the abbey. Her stark white legs, her thighs, the gray tunics, her tears. Very pale, Emma looks on: it's her own body that is being broken here, and she is elated by it. Theodelin, who has come out from the choir, looks too; when he rushes forward Emma repulses him with her crop and tramples him; her horse's hoof has broken his thigh. The demons preside in the forests: they have stepped down from their seats and are plying their trade. When it's over, Emma looks at the white priory which she took for her own body. She vanishes.

She has ridden through the wood, and left her horse at the harbor. It's already five o'clock in winter, she can hear the evening psalms being sung up above. Torches are running hither and thither in the forest, people searching for her. The moon is tiny. She unties a barge and reaches the current in the river. Her elation hasn't left her: she is laughing, her soul thirsting for obedience to a sinister fate. She disrobes, throws velvets and fur-lined cloak into the water. Around her waist she has kept the sign, the two hands' width of tightened boar hide. It was a sign, but she read it wrong. It wasn't God's boar. It was a boar that begat Gaucelin, begat the ancient altar, begat the priory, begat the charters and the viscountess of Thouars, begat crime, and is about to beget her death. It was Emma's boar. The spire above the choir gleams in the moonlight; a monastery is not a woman any more than a boar is an envoy from God. She is also elated by her mistakes, and she can see the truth alongside them, stripped of signs. All things are mutable and close to uncertain. She throws herself into the water; she sinks to the bottom, then into the wallow of the mud where she will never be found.

Or else, on the following day, she is washed up downriver on the shore of the island of Champagné, near a village of yokels whom Pierre describes as cruel, unbiddable, and barbarous. The yokel who finds her goes to fetch one of the boathooks used to haul in big fish; he returns with a few other men, and using the tip of the boathook they push the body back into the current, bloated like a leather bottle and still with the pig hide that has almost sliced it in two. They wonder whether it's a man, a woman or a pig. They laugh. The leather bottle is swept away downstream.

III

It is once again to Petrus Malleacensis—who wrote his *Chronicle* under the rule of Goderan, the fourth abbot of Maillezais, also appointed from Cluny, the saltworks of the earth, at a time when he (Pierre) was growing old, for he took his vows under the abbacy of Theodelin, lived through the exceptionally long abbacy of Humbert, and was still there, effective and in full possession of his wits since Goderan chose him for this long-term undertaking—in other words, to the inexhaustible *Chronicle of Maillezais* and also to the *Intransitive Chronicles* of Adémar de Chabannes, whom posterity knows better than Pierre, a delightful and ambitious man of letters, something of a forger, and a Limousin by birth, who oversaw a faked, devious, incontrovertible *Life of Saint Martial*, to these two authors, the one obscure and the other renowned, that I owe the following history.

Young Pierre, the scribe, is on the road to Charroux with some ten black monks on muleback in the dreary countryside, for Adémar says that it's October, and it's hard to make out the monks, blurred by the driving rain, for Adémar also mentions that it was a year of excessive rains, when the rivers burst their banks. Theodelin is riding one of the mules. He's old. He has raised buildings, fought for power, and kept it; he had Guillaume Fierabras in the palm of his hand, where he now has his son Guillaume, the Great, but he's not tired, he's enchanted by this trip to Charroux in the pouring rain. He appears to me in the form of a small, swarthy man whose hair is scarcely grayed, brusque, expansive, and brooding by turns, who limps a little when he is not on muleback. Pierre says he is a Hebrew by nation but clothed in Gallic piety, by which he doubtless means excessively preoccupied with detail, as converts are, persnickety about ritual, and, since he was born among the nation that has no idols, particularly idolatrous, with the specific idolatry that is tolerated and blessed by the saltworks of Cluny, the one devoted to saints, their lives, and their remains.

The era, as we know, loves bones. Not all bones—they're careful to choose; they argue and sometimes kill one another over these choices: only the bones that can be arrayed in a text— the Text written a thousand years ago, or the texts written a hundred years previously, or the text that was written for them the minute before—the bones that Cluny or Saint-Denis have named and sealed, those that, according to patently visible signs which are now illegible to us, were once part of a human frame from which the word of God emanated, the human frame of a saint. How they decided that one bone was to be dressed and named, displayed in gold before the eyes of men, and that another, anonymous and naked, was fit only for the blind earth we cannot understand, and only the words *cynicism* or *utter credulity* come to mind, but certainly not the words *knowledge* and *truth.* We gawp at these reliquaries in the depths of cold churches (you have to place a coin in a slot for them to emerge from the shadows), we gawp at the little notice that summarizes the saint's life which is always fundamentally the same one; the nuances escape us as they have escaped the writer of the notice; we are bored long before the little bulb goes out, the black calcium carbonates glimpsed through the grimy little window revolt us—and the artistry of the reliquaries is not particularly complicated, despite the thickness of the catalogues intent on proving that it is. We've seen the signs which no longer signify. But as we step out into the sunshine and look toward the carpark in front of the church, if five o'clock is striking in the tower above our heads, or if a few birds fly up or a wing mirror dazzles us, a mixed elation takes hold of us because on this same portico in the sunshine the thing we cannot understand—the bone and the gold and the written words all mixed together—was brandished by cynical or knowledgeable prelates before credulous or genuine crowds who were deeply affected by it. Inside the car we leaf through the thick catalogue of national museums which we do believe in, whether out of cynicism or credulity. We drive off in the October sunshine, and in an October downpour Theodelin and his monks arrive at Charroux.

There's a great gathering of bones. Martial has been brought from Limoges, his skeleton complete right down to the last metacarpal, as Adémar ensured; Valérie, whose head is all there is; and also the head alone of Saint Hilaire, the arms of Saint Stephen which were broken by stones, and many others. But all these bones matter only for their number: they've been brought to worship and vouch for an extraordinary bone, a bone from before the New Covenant, before the Text itself, the intact skull of John the Baptist, the specimen displayed on the platter in Machaerus when Salome danced and Herod drank. All the relics are there in the choir, but not the extraordinary head; it's been locked away no one knows where, the better to reveal it at the Feast of the Nativity of Saint John the Baptist, five days before All Souls'. All the prelates in the world are there, all the abbots in black, the kings—Robert, king of France, and the king of Aragon, Sancho of Navarre—all the dukes and the counts, and each day the great and powerful men of this world walk with their relics through the marveling rain-soaked crowds from Poitou, the Limousin, and Aquitaine. The head of the Baptist was found by Abbot Audouin of Angély during the demolition of the old entrance to his basilica, which was collapsing: the masons came to fetch him and led him to a stone chest set into the stone of the entrance, but of a different kind. The chest was opened, and inside there was a plain silver ball, the top of which could be lifted off, as it duly was, to reveal a skull and these words written on the inside of the lid: *Here reposes the head of the Forerunner.* Outside in the rain people are waiting patiently for the head.

It's the fifth day before All Souls'. The rain is also waiting for the great Builder, the Vienne has burst its banks, the crowds which gathered well before dawn are wading through an un-bridled River Jordan. Finally the prelates arrive with the kings, the crowd pulls back, they enter the basilica, and its doors close. Theodelin and his scribe are among their number, with the great abbots in black. The pedunculated silver ball appears between the hands of the archbishop of Bordeaux; he lifts off the lid, and the scribe sees the cranial skullcap of the illiterate saint who had a way with words. The archbishop gently removes the skull: it's there, in its entirety, with its dead man's teeth. It's placed on the altar, smoke rises from the incense, the chants start up, the bells ring out, and outside the multitudes rage. The doors open, the head brandished aloft appears on the portico. The crowds, wide-eyed, clamor, those at the back are unable to see properly because of the rain, the weighty monster which presides over the depths of the masses starts to move, those at the front climb the steps so as not to be crushed, the skull and the archbishop beat a retreat, and all the ordinary folk from the Limousin and Aquitaine, from Poitou, charge with their monster's weight from the Vienne to the church. The clerks and the kings create a rampart for the relic with their bodies, men trampled underfoot scream—and chance has driven Theodelin and Pierre right up against the altar, right up against John the Baptist. Pierre then sees the following: Theodelin deftly opens the dead man's jaw, takes hold of a tooth at the back which is slightly loose, wrenches it out, and hides it inside his own mouth. The clerks and the kings have finally cleared the door at the back and flee with the relic. Theodelin carries off the mouth with golden words inside his own mouth.

Pierre says that he never knew whether the abbot saw that Pierre had seen him.

■

At Maillezais they are short of relics: all they have is a yokel right at the bottom of the sainted hierarchy, Rogomer, whose remains were made over to them by the count of Tours and reluctantly conceded by Cluny to be holy. Throughout the return journey, Theodelin, brooding, thinks about the destiny he needs to ascribe to this powerful bone which lies against his tongue and on which another tongue once rested in order to vociferate in the wilderness. Although his abbey is the most powerful in the gulf, the best built, the whitest, it is not powerful enough to flaunt the theft in the face of Angély, which is equally powerful. To say that the Forerunner lost a tooth at Maillezais would stretch all credulity. He will have to wait.

The tooth disappears.

Adémar didn't even notice its disappearance in Charroux, Pierre hasn't seen it since Theodelin filched it, and he won't see it again until much later: the chronicles are no use to me here; I shall go in search of it myself.

Theodelin has also always been in the habit of disappearing for a while: he hands the keys over to the prior, climbs into a boat, and pushes off downstream. The monks are used to it and do not comment. They know more or less where he goes: it's that time in history; he goes on retreats in the wilderness—in this case on the easternmost island in the bay (more of an islet), which raises a steep and jagged prow toward the sea but whose stern settles onto a long sandy slope where you can land, the Île de Grues. There's not a living soul on it, scarcely any trees; the wind blows across it and sweeps down the valley of the River Lay. In winter, as now, the marshes disappear beneath the forthright sea—except for the reclaimed land that lies, just across to the south and almost within earshot, on the other eastward island, the other abbey on the gulf, Saint-Michel-en-l'Herm. On the higher part of the island, in the middle of a chaotic scattering of rocks, Theodelin has built himself a roof of wooden planks and a bed of sand, from where he can hear the sea and the wind without suffering their effects. The sea is like the sands of Egypt. It's true that Theodelin no longer really believes in the wilderness and the mortifications of Jerome and Martin, and this makes him uneasy; on the other hand, he knows that language is re-created in this windswept solitude, it recovers its focus and its fulcrum, so that on his return it cuts clean through the chatter of the monks and decisively slaps down all the blustering little monads with the Universal Monad. This is where he has come in this month of November with the tooth of John the Baptist in his mouth or in a little leather pouch, depending on his mood.

John the Baptist is returning to the wilderness.

The fishermen bring his pittance, or a monk from Saint-Michel, whose cellars are well stocked. Most often the purveyor

is Hugues, a young and sturdy brother. His large body is awkward—not that he knocks over the things he has in his hand, but
as if the things he is holding and the gesture itself were suspended in the void. It's the same with the way he speaks. He's
the opposite of a chatterer: he never remarks on the salted herring or the bread that he unloads, never offers any explanation if
today it's fresh sardines or gruel instead; he never comments
either on what's happening at Saint-Michel, the mandates, the
betrayals, the boredom or the joy as one day follows the next. If
he's asked a question, he stammers a little and blushes. But if,
while the younger man is carrying his herring up to the hut,
Theodelin takes it upon himself to remark in misty weather that
the sea and the sky are as hard to disentangle as the Chaos and
the Void, or to point out the shape of an ox in the clouds which
gradually turns into a man and is sliced in two, then Hugues
abruptly sets down his keg of herring and begins to speak, without the hint of a stutter. He says, No, what he sees is more like
the shape of a stag, and of a woman sliced in two, and though
you might think the sea and the clouds are not disentangled,
they nevertheless are, since they're the flesh and the spirit. He
can talk like this for hours on end—you just have to prompt him
from time to time—then he stops all of a sudden, embarrassed
and as if to apologize. He names only those things that can be
interpreted and gradually extended to cover the entire world,
things that you can match and substitute with words. He's not a
chatterer, but a born preacher, and he doesn't know it. Although
Hugues is very thin, tall, and covered in a thick pelt of hair,

whereas the other man is stocky and already bald, Theodelin likes to link him in his mind with Pierre, his scribe. He's like the opposite twin: he speaks the way the other man writes, in a strange mixed state of awkwardness and elation. And it satisfies neither of them, the scribe or the word-spinner.

He has already come several times this winter. As secrets are hard to keep, and as Theodelin is itching to confess, at each visit he has suggested something to Hugues which one way or another might set him on the trail of John the Baptist—and it's not at all difficult: the paths where one man always precedes another, the goatskin which you wear in winter over your black habit, the interminable baptism of the rain, a dove flying past in a brief spell of sunshine, the decapitated clouds, everything comes back to John the Baptist, the Forerunner, the Supplanted, the man who spoke loud and strong and who, because of his words, was sliced in two in Machaerus on the shores of the Dead Sea. One day in January the sea is wailing like a small child beneath a leaden sky, which may be threatening snow; everything in the bay stands out very clearly, sharply delineated, each emerging for what it is, separate, and this distresses Theodelin, who is separate and alone like a small child. He can feel his old injuries, the broken thigh from long ago, the betrayal of his former race, remorse. The boat arrives; it's Hugues bringing a ham in a sack for the last days before Lent. Without a word they walk up the path with the sack; Theodelin limps along in front; they enter the hole with its rock walls and its roof of wooden planks, where the fire is lit. Hugues takes out the ham and hangs it up by the fire, Theodelin goes over to the little altar which bears a crucifix, picks up a small leather pouch, and in front of Hugues takes out a tooth—it might have fallen out of his own mouth the minute before—he says it's a tooth belonging to John the Baptist.

After the astonishment and the excitement, the prayers, Theodelin recounts the whole thing: the rain in Charroux, the treasure stolen from under the noses of Odilon of Cluny and Robert of France, which makes them laugh, the diplomatic wait before revealing the treasure in the broad light of day and attracting alms to Maillezais. He says he doesn't trust his monks, who pry and chatter; he says, "The treasure will remain here, and there's no one worthier than you to watch over the Forerunner." He feels relieved of a great burden; the sea below has stopped wailing like a small child, it's making the noise of the sea. Hugues swears on the relic that he will speak of it to no one, that he will not steal it, that he will take care of it right here, that he will glorify it. They place the leather pouch in a little pinewood box and bury it in a place they both know beneath a larch. As the boat moves off, Theodelin hears Hugues talking to himself in a loud, strong voice. He thinks he can hear "Art thou he that should come, or do we look for another?" Theodelin leaves before Lent.

He returns at the end of the following winter. The tooth is still there. The monks in Saint-Michel have seen the smoke rising from the hut; it won't be long before they come—they take to the water with logs, bread, and fish. It's Hugues who carefully unloads the baskets of logs and who has changed: his hair is longer, he's more emaciated but seems younger, radiant. Theodelin is most astonished when, without the hint of a stutter, the other man apologizes that it's mostly chestnut wood, which burns with an infernal noise and sparks—but this year has been cold; they've had to burn a lot of wood to keep the monastery warm, and there's only chestnut left. And chestnut wood is a topic worthy of mention. In the hut he remarks that things will have to be mended here, cleared out there, and that he will attend to it. They go to sit under the larch and contemplate; Hugues meditatively pulls up a few weeds which are starting to grow—it's the end of March—as if it were a vegetable patch. The weeds are also worthy of being named, and he names them. This doesn't mean that he's lost his abilities as a preacher—on the contrary, he still happily expatiates on the shape of clouds, or that of the soul—but he's no longer embarrassed when he stops; he is innocent of the shape taken by the clouds or his words. The two men are still under the larch, standing side by side. Without looking at him, Hugues thanks the abbot: it's because of him that he has seen the sign which gives meaning to the world, and he's even become its protector. Theodelin understands—the relic of Saint John has performed a miracle: the world henceforth has a meaning for Hugues; there's no need to go looking for it in the clouds, although you can also seek it and find it in the clouds; meaning is everywhere, it's buried in the sand under the larch in a leather pouch.

Another time, as the purveyor is not Hugues but the steward brother, Theodelin gets him talking. The days of the abbot of

Saint-Michel are numbered, the prior is a melancholy man; there's no doubt that Hugues will be the next abbot; they've seen him transfigured during the past year, they are enthralled by his sermons; he bears the abbey on his shoulders. Theodelin thinks that the *vox clamantis in deserto* wasn't perhaps so vociferative, and certainly not melancholy, and that, as Saint Matthew says, Herod enjoyed listening to it in the prison at Machaerus.

■

The years pass; Hugues is abbot of Saint-Michel, Theodelin's hair is turning white, his old injuries have laid him low. He no longer goes into the wilderness—the tooth is still there, and he is right to trust Hugues, who can see the larch from the walls of the abbey, to intercede with Saint John on Theodelin's behalf. His ambition has lost its edge; he no longer wants to exhibit the relic for the glory of Maillezais, and if he did exhibit it, it would feel as if he were stealing it for a second time, but without the panache of the first. The two abbots see each other only on important occasions: consecrations or councils, arbitrations between counts, mitered appearances in Guillaume's bishopric at Poitiers, or the great black Chapter-General at Cluny. They are sometimes rivals, but it's rare that Theodelin wins, so sure are the other man's words of their right and of that of God. One winter, in the year the Norman duke and his nephews take Palermo, they are summoned to Angély by the order. They make the journey together, peaceably; they talk the way they used to, about the clouds, the body and the soul, chestnut trees and larches. Pierre the scribe is also on the journey; he reappears furtively on his mule behind the chestnut trees, and he takes up the tale again: he will write that Theodelin is limping badly, that he needs help with walking—but he doesn't say whether Hugues's is the arm that Theodelin leans on. The great prior of Cluny welcomes them in person, his demeanor grave. He welcomes Adémar de Chabannes, who arrives at the same time, and Adémar picks up the thread of his own narrative in his devious and romancical manner. The great prior gathers them in the basilica; the head of Saint John lies at the far end of the narthex in the spot reserved for those who have been excommunicated—the reliquary is wide open on the altar.

All things, says the prior, are mutable and close to uncertain. The deceased abbot Audouin did not come upon the head of Saint John in a stone wall. An Italian merchant at the hour of his death has publicly confessed, among other crimes, that he was a forger; it wasn't the head of the Baptist that he sold to Audouin, it was the head of another John, John of Edessa or John Golden Mouth, the orator of Antioch; and then, as the shadows of Hell crept over him, the terrified merchant cried out that it was nothing at all, just a bone. They proceed to the narthex; they cover the bone with thorns and ashes. They snuff all the candles; in the dark they say the prayers of malediction and mourning.

Back in his abbey, Abbot Hugues stops short on Sunday in the middle of his sermon. He stares at the bare flagstone in front of him. His words are once more suspended in the void—they finally fall into it, they abandon him, he breaks them off. They lie on the flagstone. He stutters out a few more words in which some of the monks think they recognize the verse from Ecclesiastes about words and wind. It's over. He sets down his stole and goes up to his cell. He will never speak again. He outlives his words for many years. He has become an ordinary monk once more, the lowest of the brothers, kept on only for what he once was. The younger generation, who never knew what he once was, wonder what to do with the silent old man who flees books, dutifully opens his mouth during the services, and pretends to sing. Eventually he is employed a great deal on the water, on the boats that ply from one end of the bay to the other, bringing logs and salt, fetching visitors from terra firma: this he can do, and he even seems to derive some pleasure from it. His eyes seek something in the water.

On the same Sunday that Hugues definitively falls silent, Theodelin does his duty. He launches a boat on the river—or rather Pierre, the scribe, launches a boat on the river, and Theodelin, leaning on his arm, climbs into it. Standing in the stern with his long pole Pierre steers them to the Île de Grues. The sea is wailing like a small child. Theodelin has difficulty stepping onto land and even more difficulty climbing up the slope. He curses and swears coarsely at Pierre, who is doing the best he can. He doesn't even glance at the old hut, which is falling to bits. Only once he's beneath the larch does he catch his breath again, lengthily. The wind from the south carries the sound of the bells from Saint-Michel across to them. With an oath Theodelin mutters something between his teeth, and the other man thinks he hears the verse from Ecclesiastes about words and wind. Sitting on the sand Theodelin shows Pierre where to dig; he unearths the little leather pouch and hands it to the abbot, who takes out the tiny bone: Pierre recognizes the tooth from Charroux, which belongs not to John the Baptist, but to no one. The abbot gets to his feet again—Pierre helps him up—they walk toward the sheer cliff which is close by and which looks out onto open sea. With an oath the abbot hurls the tooth into the water the way an angry child hurls a toy.

Or else the abbot loses interest and sits grumbling beneath the larch waiting for it to be done with. It's Pierre who hurls the tooth into the water. He doesn't see where it lands, and he comes up with the line which much later will be the last in his *Chronicle: As all things are mutable and close to uncertain.*

PIERRE MICHON was born in Creuse, France, in 1945. His first work of fiction was published in 1984, and since that time his reputation as one of the foremost contemporary French writers has become well established. He has won many prizes, including the Prix France Culture for his first book, *Small Lives*; the Prix Louis Guilloux for the French edition of *The Origin of the World*; and Prix de la Ville de Paris in 1996 for his body of work. He has also received the Grand Prix du Roman de l'Académie française for his novel *The Eleven*, the Grand Prix Société des gens de lettres de France (SGDL) for Lifetime Achievement in 2004, and the Prix Décembre (2002) and Petrarca-Preis (2010).

ANN JEFFERSON is Professor of French Literature at the University of Oxford and has translated work by a number of contemporary French writers.

Printed and bound by CPI Group (UK) Ltd, Croydon, CR0 4YY

13/04/2025

14656467-0001